South Shore Billionaires

Billionaires finding brides!

Bonded at boarding school, best friends Jeremy, Branson and Cole have scaled the world's rich lists and become New York's wealthiest tycoons.

Now these billionaires are swapping the bright lights of the city for the blue waters and golden sands of the coast. In stunning South Shore, they'll find love and taste a life they never knew they wanted!

Read Jeremy's story in

Christmas Baby for the Billionaire

Discover Branson's story in

Beauty and the Brooding Billionaire

And look out for Cole's story

Coming soon!

Dear Reader,

Welcome back to the South Shore Billionaires! In the previous book, *Christmas Baby for the Billionaire*, we saw Jeremy find happiness. Now it's time to set our sights on Bran.

Bran's got a lot of healing to do. He's suffered some big losses in his life. He's a bestselling author who hasn't been able to write since tragedy struck. But along comes Jessica Blundon, with her sunny hair and sunny smiles and stubborn spirit. Before long Bran finds himself wanting to rejoin the land of the living. And who knows...maybe the words will start flowing again!

Writing through hard times can be a real challenge. As a writer, sometimes strife is what drives us to lose ourselves in the stories we create. But sometimes it also has the opposite effect, and creating seems utterly impossible. That's so difficult.

But you know, the sun comes out again, and somewhere along the way we find our way back to joy. And that's the best feeling in the world. It gave me a lot of joy to write this story for two characters who certainly deserved happiness.

I do hope you enjoy Branson and Jessica's story, and come back for Cole's own happy-ever-after, coming soon!

Best wishes,

Donna

Beauty and the Brooding Billionaire

Donna Alward

ISBN-13: 978-0-373-XXXXX-X

Beauty and the Brooding Billionaire

Copyright © 2016 by Donna Alward

HARLEQUIN

Romance

Recycling programs
for this product may
not exist in your area.

ISBN-13: 978-1-335-55615-8

Beauty and the Brooding Billionaire

Copyright © 2020 by Donna Alward

This edition published by arrangement with Harlequin Books S.A.

For questions and comments about the quality of this book,
please contact us at CustomerService@Harlequin.com.

Harlequin Enterprises ULC
22 Adelaide St. West, 40th Floor
Toronto, Ontario M5H 4E3, Canada
www.Harlequin.com

Printed in U.S.A.

Donna Alward lives on Canada's east coast with her family, which includes her husband, a couple of kids, a senior dog and two crazy cats. Her heartwarming stories of love, hope and homecoming have been translated into several languages, hit bestseller lists and won awards, but her favorite thing is hearing from readers! When she's not writing she enjoys reading (of course), knitting, gardening, cooking... and she is a *Masterpiece Theatre* addict. You can visit her on the web at donnaalward.com and join her mailing list at donnaalward.com/newsletter.

Books by Donna Alward

Harlequin Romance

South Shore Billionaires

Christmas Baby for the Billionaire

Destination Brides

Summer Escape with the Tycoon

Marrying a Millionaire

Best Man for the Wedding Planner
Secret Millionaire for the Surrogate

Heart to Heart

Hired: The Italian's Bride

Visit the Author Profile page
at Harlequin.com for more titles.

Praise for
Donna Alward

"Ms. Alward wrote a wonderfully emotional story
that is not to be missed. She provided a tale
rich with emotions, filled with sexual chemistry,
wonderful dialogue, and endearing characters....
I highly recommend *Summer Escape with the
Tycoon* to other readers."

—*Goodreads*

CHAPTER ONE

JESS TOOK ONE look at the lighthouse and knew that the search had been worth it. After weeks of wandering, and months before that of her pencils hovering over her sketch pad, the battered white-and-red lighthouse on Nova Scotia's east coast stood firm against the brisk, briny wind.

In some regards she wondered if the lonely structure *was* her. Tall, a bit battered from the winds of life, but still standing.

Her agent was after her to do another show. "Your last one was such a success," Jack had insisted. "An original Jessica Blundon commands top dollar right now."

"You can't rush the muse," she'd replied, deliberately keeping her voice light. "I don't paint to order."

She hadn't been painting at all. Not since Ana's death. Her mentor. Her best friend. The older sister she'd never had. Losing Ana had devastated her and killed her creativity. Her life had suddenly become colorless and empty. No significant other. No children. No best friend.

She'd isolated herself far too much. So after a good year of grieving and moping, she'd decided to stop hiding away and go in search of what her life was going to look like. The best place to start, she figured, was finding her passion to paint again.

And while she didn't "paint to order," she did do this as her career. Like most creatives, it was impossible to separate what she did from who she was.

The biggest shock had been that when she was finally ready to put brush to canvas, she couldn't. The block had been real and infuriating, until about six months ago, when she'd finally started sketching.

And traveling. She'd left behind the waters of the Great Lakes—Chicago—and gone west, to Seattle first, then San Francisco and down the coast to San Diego. The Pacific had been beautiful, but it wasn't what she was looking for. She was searching for that feeling, right in her solar plexus, that told her when something was just *right*. The Gulf of Mexico hadn't been it, either, though she'd adored her time in New Orleans and along the panhandle. She'd come closer to finding "it" the farther north she'd gone; past the barrier islands in the Carolinas, to the beaches of New Jersey and then the rugged coastline of Maine. On a whim she'd jumped on the CAT ferry in Bar Harbor and headed to Canada. She'd sketched lonely beaches, colorful coastal houses, gray rocks made black by the ocean waves. Trees budding in the mild spring weather. All lovely. But nothing that had felt inspiring. Nothing that created the burn to create.

Her sketchbook was full of drawings, but the lighthouse before her? It was that punch-to-the-gut feeling, and she relished the trickle of excitement running through her veins. "This is it, Ana," she murmured. "It's time."

The brisk wind off the ocean tossed her hair around her face and bit through the light cotton shirt she wore. May was definitely not Nova Scotia's warmest month, even though the sun shone brightly and warmed a spot between her shoulder blades. She needed to get a different vantage point. The angle here was too sharp. But the lighthouse stood on a bluff jutting out toward the sea, and the only path to it seemed to be from the property before her. And the gate that baldly pronounced Private Property—Do Not Enter.

"Private property," she grumbled, peering over the metal barrier. She couldn't see the house from here, and the drive led to the left while the lighthouse was off to the right and then south. Lips set, she swung her bag over her shoulder and put her foot on the bottom railing of the gate.

"Not electric." She grinned and then nimbly hoisted herself over the metal railings and landed on the other side.

It didn't take long for her to get a glimpse of the house. It was an imposing but beautiful structure, with gray siding and stonework and what would be marvelous gardens in another month or so. Fledgling hostas, their leaves still tightly furled, and a variety of tulips and hyacinths kept the beds from looking sad and naked. Jess expected that there were other perennials beneath the surface waiting for the summer warmth to wake them. The house had a fantastic panoramic view of the Atlantic coastline, and a sloped lawn led to what appeared to be low cliffs. She wondered if there was a beach below. And she'd like to look, but first she wanted to skirt the property and get to the isolated lighthouse, so she could take some pictures and perhaps make a sketch or two.

The ground was hard and rocky beneath her feet as she set off to the lonely tower. She'd made a friend at the nearby resort, and Tori had told her about the hidden gem, suggesting its semi-neglected state might add to its allure. She hadn't been wrong. The weather-beaten clapboards on the outside were in sad need of fresh paint, and as Jess got closer, she realized that the gray wood was worn surprisingly smooth from wind and salt. There was rust on the hinges of the door, and she wondered if the thing would even open or what she might find inside if it did. Dirt? Mice? Other creatures? She looked way up to the top, where the beacon lay, silent and still. Did it still work?

The lighthouse was full of character and secret stories. Her favorite kind of subject.

After her cursory examination, she pulled out her camera and started taking shots. Different angles, distances, close-ups, and with the Atlantic in the background. The ocean was restless today, and she loved the whitecaps that showed in her viewfinder, and the odd spray from waves that crashed on the rocks below.

After she took the photos, she thought she might like to get a few of the house, too. It was more modern and certainly very grand, but still with that lonely brave-the-elements esthetic that she loved. She swung around toward the property and came face-to-face with a pair of angry eyes. The man they belonged to gave her a real start.

"You're trespassing," he said, his voice sharp and condemning.

He looked like a hermit. It was hard to tell his age, because his hair was shaggy and his beard was in dire need of trimming, but she guessed maybe forty, or a little older. The brown shirt was wrinkled and slightly too big for his lean frame, and he wore faded jeans and worn boots. All in all, he was a little bit intimidating. Not just his looks, but the expression on his face. He was angry, and he wasn't bothering to hide it.

Somehow, though, she found him rather compelling. Rugged and mysterious, and beneath the scruff his looks were quite appealing. She rather thought she'd like to sketch him. And while he was intimidating, he didn't seem… dangerous. Just grouchy.

"I was only on the property for a few minutes. I stayed right along the edge until I got to the lighthouse."

"The lighthouse *is* on my property. I'm assuming you saw the sign, and chose to ignore it."

She didn't have an answer to that, because it was true. Except she hadn't realized that the lighthouse was on his private property. Weren't they usually parkland or municipal or something? How many people owned their very own lighthouse?

She put on her most contrite face. Despite his abrasive manner, it appeared she was in the wrong here, not him. If she wanted to have access to this perfect aspect, she needed to appeal to his...friendly side? If he had one.

"I'm really sorry. I truly didn't realize the lighthouse was part of your property. I'm an artist, you see. I'd heard about it from someone at the Sandpiper Resort, and they assured me it was worth checking out. I wouldn't have trespassed if I had realized I wasn't just, well, cutting across your lot."

He crossed his arms.

Now she was getting annoyed. Had she done anything so very awful that meant he had to be so...disagreeable?

She tried again. "I'm Jessica Blundon." She held out her hand and smiled.

He didn't shake it. Instead, his dark eyes assessed her from top to bottom, making her feel...lacking. One of his eyebrows lifted slightly, a question mark. She held his gaze, refusing to cower. If his goal was to intimidate her, he was failing. Despite his horrible manners, she did not feel the least bit threatened. This dog's bark was worse than his bite, she figured. There was something in his gaze that she responded to. He wanted to be left alone. It wasn't long ago she'd felt the same, so she merely lowered her hand and wondered what was hidden behind the beard and longish hair and grumpy exterior.

"Well, Miss Blundon, you're on private property. I'll ask you to delete those photos off your camera and go back to where you came from."

Her mouth dropped open. He was actually going to get her to delete her pictures? She closed her mouth and frowned. "Is that really necessary? I mean, it's not like the lighthouse is some giant secret."

"It's my lighthouse, on my property, and I don't want you to have pictures of it." He reached into his pocket and took out a cell phone. "You can delete them or I can make a phone call and have the cops out here."

Now he was being utterly unreasonable, and any curiosity or sympathy she'd felt fled. "I could walk away and take my pictures with me. Unless you're planning to personally restrain me."

She lifted her chin, met his gaze. Something flared there, and nerves skittered along her spine. Not of fear. But of awareness. Mr. Hermit was enigmatic, and no matter how much he tried to hide behind his ragged appearance, he was actually quite attractive. There was something familiar about him, too, that she couldn't quite place.

His gaze dropped to her lips, then back up again to her eyes, and for the first time, his mouth curved in a slight smile. "Good luck," he replied. "I know your name and I know you're at the Sandpiper. Not too hard to tell the RCMP where to look."

He'd call the Mounties. He'd really do it, over a few stupid pictures. She lifted her camera and glared at him. "Fine. I'll delete the damned pictures." Her heart broke a little bit just saying it. She needed them. The first true inspiration she'd had in two years...darn it. She held his gaze and got the sense he wasn't bluffing.

"You could just give me the memory card."

"I don't think so. It wasn't blank when I got here. I'll delete the ones I took just now but that's all. And you're being a jerk."

He shrugged. "I've been called worse."

Jessica switched to view mode and with growing frustration started deleting all the beautiful pictures she'd already taken, all the while calling him worse in her mind. He was being completely unreasonable. She toyed with the idea of keeping one or two, trying to hide them from him, but then figured why bother. When she looked up, he held out his hand.

"Oh, for Pete's sake," she muttered, taking the strap off her neck and putting the camera in his hands.

He scrolled through, appeared to be satisfied, and handed it back.

"Thank you. You can leave now."

Her cheeks flared at being so readily dismissed. She shoved the camera into her tote, fuming. He hadn't even offered his name when she'd introduced herself.

She met his gaze. "For the record, you didn't have to be so rude."

Then she swept by him. She was only a few feet away when she thought she heard him say, "Yes, I did." But when she looked over her shoulder, he was standing with his back to her, looking out to sea.

She hurried on, but when she got to a curve in the property, she turned back. He was still standing in the same spot, looking angry and lonely and lost.

She reached for her camera and took one hurried shot, then scurried back to the gate.

Bran sensed when she was completely gone, and let out a low breath.

Solitude. All he wanted was solitude. For people to leave him alone. The months of pretending in New York had taken their toll. He'd lost himself in his grief, only pulled out occasionally by his best friends, Cole and Jeremy. There'd even been times when he'd smiled and laughed. But then he'd gone home to the reminders of the life he'd once had, the one he'd been on the cusp of having, and he'd fallen apart. Every. Single. Time.

When he'd started to self-medicate with alcohol, he'd known he had to make a change. At first it had been just beer, and in the words of his grandmother, "it's not alcoholism if it's beer." He'd used that for a long time to justify his overindulgence. But when he'd graduated to Scotch, and then whatever alcohol was available, he'd known he was in trouble. He needed to sell the brownstone and get away from the constant reminders. Get his act together.

Jennie would be so angry to know that he'd resorted to alcohol to cope. And so he'd thrown out all the booze, because Jennie's memory deserved better.

The house in Nova Scotia was damned near perfect. Sometimes Jeremy and his new wife were close by, providing him with the odd company to keep him from transitioning from eccentric to downright crazy. No one knew him here, or if they did recognize his name, they didn't make a big time about it. He had groceries delivered to the house. Couriers delivered anything he could buy online…there wasn't much shopping nearby anyway. He spent hours staring out at the sea, trying to make sense of everything. Wondering how to stop caring.

Wondering if he'd ever be able to write again.

The one downside was the stupid lighthouse. In the beginning, it had been an incentive to buy. It was interesting and unusual, and he'd liked the idea of owning it. What he hadn't counted on was the foot traffic, skirting his property and solitude with cameras and picnic blankets and... He shuddered. At least once a week he found a condom on the ground. It wasn't so much the idea of it being the site for romantic trysts. He could appreciate a romantic atmosphere. But heck, would it be too much to ask for people to pick up after themselves?

Today he'd seen the reddish-blond head, and he'd had enough. The moment she'd pulled out her camera and started taking photos, he was ready to put on his boots. But when she turned to take a picture of the house? That was the clincher. He valued his privacy far too much. So far reporters hadn't found him, as they had in New York. But it was only a matter of time. She didn't seem like a journalist or a paparazzo, but he couldn't be sure.

He watched a gull buffeted by the wind and sighed. She was right; he'd been a jerk about it. And part of that was because she'd been trespassing, and the other part was because he'd immediately realized how pretty she was. Early thirties, he'd guess, with blue eyes that had golden-green stripes through the irises, making them a most unusual color that deepened when she got angry, as she'd been with him when he'd demanded she delete her pictures. A dusting of freckles dotted her nose, pale, but enough that it made her look younger than she was. But there were shadows there, too. And the fact that he'd been curious at all set him on edge.

He started back to the house, turning over the encounter in his mind. Jessica Blundon, she'd said. The name sounded vaguely familiar, but he wasn't sure why. Maybe she was a reporter.

Once inside, he went to his "den," a round-shaped room on the bottom floor of the house with windows all the way around. There was a fireplace there for when it was cold or damp, as it had often been during the end of the winter when he'd moved in. A huge bookcase was near the door, the shelves jammed with a mixture of keepers, books on writing and stories he had yet to read. The furniture was heavy and well-cushioned, perfect for curling up with a book. He picked up his laptop and hit the power button, then started an internet search.

It wasn't difficult to find her. The first hit was her website, and the second was for a gallery in Chicago. Her site had her picture on a press page, but also a catalog of her paintings. He wiped a hand over his face. She was good. Really good. The gallery page brought up a press release from a showing she'd done…nearly two years ago. He flipped back to her site. It didn't appear to have been updated recently.

Had she not been painting all this time? Or had she been secluded away, working on something new?

Something sharp slid through him, and he recognized it as envy. He wasn't sure he'd ever feel whole enough to write again, and his agent had got him an indefinite extension of his contract, with his publisher saying he could turn in a manuscript when he wanted. Hell, at this point his publisher had more faith in him than he did in himself. The only thing keeping him from paying back the advance and killing the deal was that he was in his thirties. What else was he going to do with his life? At least with the open contract, there was something left ahead for him. More than just picking away at his trust fund, and existing.

And here *she* was, with her messy hair and bright eyes and pink cheeks, living life and standing up to the ogre.

Because that was surely what he'd become, and he hated himself for it.

But he was certain he didn't deserve any better.

He lowered the cover of the laptop and set it aside, then picked up his coffee and took a cold sip.

He'd stopped drinking. But nothing else had changed. And that scared him to death.

Jessica looked around the gardens of Jeremy and Tori's house and let out a happy sigh. The property didn't have the wild restlessness of the one with the lighthouse, but the scent of the ocean was strong and the burgeoning perennials added bursts of color. Tori had invited her to dinner, and now they sat outside, listening to the ocean and having tea. Tori held her three-week-old baby in her arms, the tiny bundle making small noises as she slept. Jessica held back the spurt of jealousy. She'd had a chance at a husband and family once, and had blown it. She'd been all of twenty-four and had wanted to travel and paint and not settle down yet.

He hadn't waited. Broken heart number one.

Now she was in her thirties with no relationship on the radar. She'd started to accept that a partner and family was not in the cards for her. It seemed that everyone important in her life always picked up and left in one way or another, and after a while a heart got tired of taking all the risks and never reaping the rewards.

It didn't stop her from getting wistful and broody around Tori's newborn, though. And when Tori asked if she'd hold the baby while she popped inside for a light blanket, Jessica had no choice but to say yes.

Little Rose was a porcelain doll, with pale skin and thick lashes and a dusting of soft, brown hair. Her little lips sucked in and out as she slept, and she smelled like baby lotion. Jess cradled her close, looking down at her face and marveling at the feel of the warm weight in the crook of her arm. She did like babies. A lot.

When Tori came back, Jess held out her hand for the blanket, unwilling to give the baby up just yet. "She's comfortable here and it'll give you a break."

"You mean I'll get to drink my tea while it's hot?"

Jess chuckled. "Exactly." She tucked the crocheted blanket around the baby and leaned back in the chair. "Thank you again for asking me to dinner. The food at the inn is lovely, but a home-cooked meal was very welcome."

"It wasn't anything fancy."

They'd had salad, grilled chicken and some sort of barley and vegetable side dish that had been delicious. Jeremy was now inside, catching up on some work while they enjoyed the spring evening.

"It was delicious. Besides, I was hungry. Someone made me angry today, and I went for a run on the beach after to burn off some steam."

Tori leaned forward. "Angry? Who? Not one of the staff, I hope."

Tori had resigned her position at the Sand-piper Resort, but she was still close with the staff and popped in on occasion to help with events or answer any questions the new assistant manager had. That was how Tori and Jess had met, and they'd ended up chatting and then sharing lunch on the resort patio.

"No, not staff. You know the lighthouse you told me about? I went to see it. Get some pictures…it's gorgeous, just like you said. I got that tingly feeling I haven't had in a really long time. And then the owner showed up. Man, he was a jerk."

She expected Tori to express her own form of outrage, but instead her eyes danced. "So you met Bran."

"You know him? Like, personally?"

"He's Jeremy's friend."

Jess lifted an eyebrow. "You might have warned me. What an ogre. Hard to imagine him being friendly to anyone."

Yet even as she said it she recalled the flash of vulnerability in his eyes. And while his hair was in major need of a haircut, it had been thick and wavy, a rich brown tossed by the sea breeze. Roguish.

"Bran's been through a lot. He just moved here in February, too. The house is lovely, isn't it?"

"I didn't get to see much of anything. I took some pictures of the lighthouse, and then he stomped out and growled at me and made me delete all the photos I'd taken."

Tori frowned. "He's usually not quite that grumpy."

"He was downright rude." She sighed. "That lighthouse was it. I got the rush I get when I'm particularly inspired. If I could have kept one photo, I could have at least started a sketch."

Except she did have one photo. The one she'd taken of "Bran," now that she knew his name. Facing the ocean. She'd looked at it after her run, and had felt his loneliness.

Something else jiggled in her memory. "You said his name was Bran?"

"Short for Branson." Tori leaned forward. "Do you want me to take her now?" She held out her hands for the baby.

"She's asleep and fine here as long as you're okay with it."

"Are you kidding? When she's sleeping I get to relax." She sat back in her chair. "I just don't want to take advantage."

Jessica turned the name over and over in her mind. Branson. The dark hair, the eyes…

"Branson Black," she said, her voice a bit breathy. "That's him, isn't it? The author?"

Tori frowned. "He keeps a very low profile here. No one in town really knows who he is."

"Of course. It'd be like having Stephen King as your neighbor."

Tori laughed. "Not quite. He's not that famous."

Jess tucked the blanket closer around the baby. "He's pretty famous. And he hasn't published anything since—"

She halted. She remembered the story now. Since his wife and infant son had died in a car crash.

It all came together now. His isolation. Desolation. Growling to keep people away. He was buried in grief, a feeling she could relate to oh, so well. A pit opened in her stomach, a reminder of the dark days she'd had after Ana's death. And a well of sympathy, too. How devastated he must be.

She met Tori's gaze and sighed. "It was in the news."

Tori nodded. "I don't want to betray a confidence, you understand. But yes, he's been struggling with his grief."

"And values his privacy. I understand now."

And her frustration melted away, replaced by sympathy.

"Do you?" Tori's eyes were sharp. "Because he's one of the best men I know. He's one of the reasons Jeremy and I are together."

Jess stared into the flickering fire. "A few years ago I lost my mentor and...well, the best friend a person could have. I'm just now starting to paint again. So yes, I get it. Grief can destroy the deepest and best parts of us if we're not careful."

Silence fell over the patio for a few minutes. Then Tori spoke up. "I'm sorry about your friend. And I agree with you. Which was why I sent you over there in the first place."

Jess's head snapped up. "You did?"

Tori nodded. "He needs someone to stir him up a bit. Looks like you did."

Jess wasn't too sure of that. But her heart gave a twist, thinking of what he'd lost, what he was suffering and how alone he must feel. Because she'd been there. And she'd come out the other side.

He hadn't. And that made her sorry indeed.

CHAPTER TWO

BRAN HAD BEEN up for a walk at dawn, made himself breakfast, had thrown in a load of laundry and was now left with most of the day stretching before him. Each day he had the same ritual. Walk, eat, some sort of menial chore. Check email. Anything to procrastinate so he wouldn't spend hours staring at an empty document. He got through those daily rituals just fine, but the moment he opened up a new file on his laptop, he froze.

He wrote mysteries, and right now, anything dealing with a murder and victims was too much. Even though Jennie and Owen had been in a highway accident and not victims of violence, he just couldn't deal with the idea of dead bodies. The grief was too much. His memory was too vivid.

Instead, he went upstairs and out on the balcony. The fresh air bit at his cheeks, carrying the tang of the ocean as the sky spread blue and wide above him. The lighthouse stood sentinel at the corner of the property, and he shoved his hands in his jeans pockets, thinking of yesterday and the woman who'd shown up uninvited.

She was right. He'd been a jerk. Right now he didn't know how to be anything else. But he was slightly sorry for it. Maybe would be more sorry if she'd been hurt by his gruffness. Instead, she'd been annoyed, and her eyes had sparked with it. It was hard to be sorry for that. She had beautiful eyes, annoyed or not.

He'd been standing there for twenty minutes when a movement caught his eye, just off the shore. He frowned. Was that a boat? He squinted; the sun glinted off the water in blinding flashes, but yes, there was definitely a boat out there, maybe a few hundred yards off the coastline. Certainly no farther. The sea was still rough, and he watched the boat bob and rock, at the mercy of the waves.

Foolish person. The boat couldn't be more than maybe fifteen, sixteen feet. On a calm day, and with a skilled pilot, a boat like that could fare pretty well in open water. He'd certainly gone fishing in his and had no trouble at all. But today wasn't calm. The surf had been high since the storm earlier in the week, and whoever was at the wheel wasn't looking very competent, either. He frowned, and turned to get his binoculars from downstairs. When he returned, the boat was closer to shore, and still bobbing as it drifted.

He lifted the binoculars, focused in, and cursed.

What in hell was she doing? Foolish woman! Out there in a boat, camera around her neck, trying to take stupid pictures! Had he not made his point? He ran his hand through his hair and lifted the binoculars once more. A rolling wave hit the boat sideways, throwing her off balance. She fell, and his heart froze for a few moments as she disappeared from view. Had she hit her head? Was she okay? He held his breath until he saw her struggling to stand again. She turned the craft into the waves, and he hoped to God that she was going to give it some gas and get out of there. But she didn't. She wanted her pictures too badly. As she lifted her camera again, another heavy wave crested and knocked her to the side, while water splashed over boat and woman. If she wasn't careful, she'd be knocked overboard. Or worse…she'd be swept in toward the jagged rocks at the point. The lighthouse was there for a reason, after all.

Another wave swamped the boat and panic settled in his gut. He took off the binoculars and raced down the stairs, out the front door, and to the natural steps leading to his beach and the private dock. It took only a few moments for him to throw on a life vest and start the engine of the boat that was only slightly bigger than hers. He drew away from the dock and opened the throttle as he made his way toward her, his heart pounding as the boat lifted and bottomed out with each rolling wave. If she wasn't swept overboard, she was going to hit the rocks, and neither outcome was particularly appealing. The water was freezing, and while he was confident in his piloting skills, he wasn't so sure about his rescue ones. The only option was to get her out of there.

He got close enough to see that Jessica's delicate pale skin was even paler, her eyes wide with fear. Her jaw tightened as she saw that he was behind the wheel, and she waved him off. "I've got this!" she called. "Go away!"

His fear disintegrated and anger took its place. "Are you kidding me?" He pulled as close as he dared without danger of them crashing together. "You're either going to fall overboard or run into those rocks! Do what I tell you."

Her face flattened. "No man is going to tell me to—"

He swore, and loudly, and Jessica's mouth clamped shut in surprise. "I'm going to tow you back," he shouted. "No arguments. Now shut up and let me help."

When she didn't argue, he figured she'd either finally seen common sense or was too scared to do otherwise. It took several minutes for them to secure her boat to his, with the ominous cliffs of the point coming ever closer. Bran gritted his teeth and pushed the throttle forward, taking up the slack between the two boats as the motor labored to take them both into the oncoming waves and away from shore. Jessica, to his relief, had finally done what he'd told her and was sitting obediently in the captain's seat. The chop smoothed out as they got closer to the tiny cove sheltering his beach, and once they got close to the dock, he stopped, put down his anchor and pulled Jessica's boat close enough he could board. She stood, avoiding his gaze, and stepped away from the wheel.

He stepped in just as a wave sent her off balance and crashing into him.

She was damp from spray, and yet warm and soft as he caught her in his arms and their bodies meshed together awkwardly. Bran put his hands on her upper arms to steady her and push her away. But the damage was done. Her gaze caught his and her cheeks—already rosy from the wind and water—reddened. His gaze dropped to her full, pink lips and his irritation grew. It was bad enough she was a thorn in his side…it was too much that she was also adorable. She bit down on her lip, and he nearly groaned. Adorable wasn't quite the right word. Infuriating and…sexy, dammit.

He pushed his way around her. After disconnecting the towrope, he guided her little boat into his dock and secured it. He left her on the wooden platform and, ignoring the freezing temperatures, dove into the water. Perhaps it would help cool his temper, which was still raging.

The icy shock definitely cleared his mind. He wasted no time climbing the little ladder into his craft, then started the engine and guided it in to the dock. Soaked and shivering, he jumped out and glared at Jessica, who was standing on the dock, looking quite chastised and embarrassingly repentant.

He would not let that get to him. He would not. He focused on tying the knot and not on her frightened face and big eyes.

"Get your things and come to the house," he ordered, and he didn't wait to see if she followed or not. She would if she had any sort of sense at all.

But he didn't check; he heard her feet scrambling up the stone steps behind him. He hurried to the house and stripped off his shirt the moment he got in the door. Within five minutes he'd dumped his wet clothes in the tub and had on warm, dry jeans. He was walking toward the front door with his sweatshirt in his hand when he stopped short.

She'd come inside, just into the foyer, and stood staring at him and his bare chest. Her cheeks blossomed an awkward shade of pink, and she bit down on her lip as he shoved his arms in the sleeves and pulled the shirt over his head. But something strange threaded through him at her silent acknowledgment of…what? Attraction? Awareness? What a ridiculous thought.

He opened the door and guided her outside again, then put a set of keys in her hand. "Where did you get the boat?"

She cleared her throat, and the awkwardness dissipated as they were back on topic. "Cummins's, about a mile from the resort."

He knew the location. "Take my car and drive there. I'll take the boat back. Then I'll drop you at the resort and that's that."

"Branson, I…"

His gaze snapped to her. "How do you know who I am?"

She didn't answer, and he held back a sigh of frustration. It had to have been Tori or Jeremy. "It doesn't matter. Take the car."

He stalked off to the dock again. Damn woman was nothing but trouble.

It took thirty minutes to get to Cummins's boat rentals, and Jessica was already there, her backpack slung over one shoulder. Bran held on to his anger as he turned the boat over to John Cummins, then followed Jessica back to where she'd parked his car. He got in the driver's side and immediately hit his knees on the steering wheel; she'd moved the seat forward. Held back another curse word as he adjusted it, and turned onto the road leading back to the Sandpiper.

He never spoke to her once.

She never spoke to him, either.

The drive was short, and he dropped her in front of reception. Then, and only then, did she speak.

"Thank you," she said quietly, and backed away from the door, as if afraid to say more.

He didn't answer. She shut the door, and he put the car in gear and steered back onto the main road.

But a hundred yards up the road, he pulled over to the side and gulped for air as the shakes finally set in.

The shakes had held on for a long time, part of an anxiety attack that had been utterly debilitating. When he'd been good to drive again, he'd eased his way home, parked the car and had stood at his front door for ten solid minutes, knowing he should go inside, unsure of what he wanted to do when he was in there. The urge for Scotch was strong, so it was just as well he didn't have any. He didn't want to be alone, but the idea of having company was repulsive. The adrenaline in his body told him to pace; the idea of lying down on his long sofa and avoiding everything held similar attraction.

She could have died. Died! For being utterly foolish.

It was just a damned lighthouse. There were dozens along the coast. She could pick another one.

If he'd let her keep her pictures yesterday, this never would have happened. And if she'd been hurt, or worse, today, that would have been his fault.

Like he didn't already have enough guilt. It was bad enough he had Jennie and Owen on his conscience. The last thing he wanted was to add to the tally of people he'd failed.

In the end he went inside and sat on the sofa, staring at the unlit fireplace. It didn't take a genius to figure out that his fear and anger were all tied up in Jennie and Owen, and how he hadn't been able to save them. Or how his selfishness was responsible for them being on the road in the first place. Jennie hated driving from their place in Connecticut into the city, but he'd been too busy to drive home to see them.

All his life he'd promised himself he'd be different from his father, who had always been too busy working to spend time with his wife and son. He'd promised himself he'd be there, and present, and cherish every moment so his kid would never feel alone or unloved. And he'd failed spectacularly.

Since he was too busy to go home, Jennie had been going to surprise him with a midweek visit while he was doing promo for his latest book.

And they'd never made it.

Jessica probably hated him. He certainly wasn't overly keen on her at the moment. But she was alive, and he'd take that as a win.

And hopefully that would be the last he'd see of her. Surely, after today, she'd learned her lesson.

Jessica felt like a complete and utter fool.

An online course and a few fun rides on the lake years ago, and she'd considered herself suitably experienced to be piloting a boat on rough waters. To Cummins's credit, he hadn't been keen on renting her the boat, but she'd assured him it was a short trip and she'd be fine. And she had been, at first. Until she got near the point at Bran's place.

She'd wanted to get the pictures and get gone. But the waves had been bigger than she'd expected, and more than once she'd hung over the side and retched. The crosscurrent had made everything more difficult, and one particular roll had knocked her down, her shoulder ramming against the fiberglass side.

It still hurt, but not as much as her pride.

She looked at the bruise forming on her shoulder and sighed, then gently put her arms in a soft sweater and pulled it over her head. The moment she'd seen Branson coming toward her, she'd been relieved and then embarrassed all at once. She didn't need rescuing, for Pete's sake. She'd never needed rescuing. She was very good at picking up when things went wrong and starting over. She'd done it when her adoptive parents had divorced. When her mom had died. When she'd lost jobs in the days before she could make a living with her art. After her horrible breakup. Even Ana hadn't rescued her...not really. She'd just appeared, ready to be a friend, a confidant, a professional mentor. She had made Jessica's life richer, but she hadn't saved it.

Today Jessica felt as if Branson Black had

literally saved her life. She'd been reckless—not unlike her. But she'd got in over her head, and he'd come to her rescue. He hadn't been pleased about it, either. He hadn't even grunted when she said thank you when he dropped her off.

Twice now she'd got off on the wrong foot with him. Instead of sneaking photos from the water and never having to deal with him again, she'd made it more obvious than ever that she was a pain in his neck.

And for that, she needed to apologize.

She had no idea how to do that, but she'd come up with something. And kill him with kindness if she had to.

Room service sounded like a perfect idea, so she ordered and then took the memory card from her camera and popped it into her laptop. When she opened up the directory and brought up the first picture, she sighed. It was out of focus, but not too bad. But there were only two or three that were even close to being useful. Then the lens got wet and every single picture was blurred and smudged.

All of that for nothing. She'd only accomplished making him hate her even more. Tomorrow she would apologize. And then she'd find another lighthouse. Or something else that sparked her creativity and gave her the burn to create again. In the meantime she'd keep working, because nothing helped get the muse back in business like being ready for her.

CHAPTER THREE

BRAN WAS DRINKING coffee on his deck when he saw someone coming through the stand of trees toward his driveway. He shifted over to the side so he'd be less conspicuous. Maybe it was Tori, or Jeremy, though they usually called first. It took only ten seconds for him to realize it was Jessica. Again? Frustration burned with the coffee in his mouth. Hadn't she caused enough trouble? What the heck was it about his lighthouse that was so intriguing, anyway?

But instead of turning toward the lighthouse, she headed straight for his front door.

Something twisted in his gut. He watched as she drew closer, carrying a paper sack in her arms, her sunshiny hair glinting in the morning sun. There was something so pure about her, so bright and light. He waited out of sight for her to go to the door; heard the knock echo both below him and through the house.

He should answer. Yesterday he'd been so

angry and hopped up on adrenaline and fear that he hadn't said anything to her other than snapping at her to take his car to the boat rental. Both their encounters had been antagonistic, but last night, as he'd sat in the twilight, he'd realized that yesterday's foolish actions could have been avoided if he'd been nicer at the start and let her keep her photos.

Because he felt that responsibility, he was trying not to be too angry with her. Letting go of his anger left room for other feelings, though. Ones he truly wasn't ready for nor desired. At the very least, discomfort at the sheer amount of time she was in his thoughts at all.

She knocked again. He should go down. And yet the idea of company, of small talk…what would he say? It was different when it was Jeremy or Cole or even Tori. And when he was out in public and didn't have to actually have conversations of any consequence. It was a hello and thank you to the cashier at the market. A thank you to the lady at the post office. What would they say…especially after yesterday?

In the end, he hesitated long enough that she abandoned the door and started back down the drive, only without the paper bag.

Whatever she'd brought with her, she'd left for him. An olive branch? And he was up here like a coward. While he wasn't feeling social, he didn't like that idea. There was nothing to be afraid of. At least today, no one was in any danger.

He stepped to the railing. "Miss Blundon."

She turned around and looked up, shading her eyes with her hand. "Oh! You're up there!"

Did she have to sound so delighted by the discovery? Surely seeing him wasn't exactly a pleasure. Not after the way he'd treated her.

"If you'll wait a few moments, I'll be right down."

"Of course." She smiled at him, a bright reward in his otherwise bleak day.

The whole way down the stairs he wondered what he was doing. He'd moved here to get away from people. To...work through his feelings without any burden of expectation. And now he was going to open the door to a red-headed sprite with eyes that snapped and a bright smile. As if yesterday had never even happened.

He'd say thank you for whatever was in the bag and send her on her way.

When he reached the door, she'd retrieved the bag and held it in her arms again, and met him with the same bright smile.

"Good morning!" she said, holding out the bag. "A peace offering for getting off on the wrong foot. Feet. Whatever. Twice."

Her babbling shouldn't have been charming. He instinctively reached for the bag, then regretted it because it meant automatic acceptance. He couched it in the crook of his arm, aimed a level stare at her and said, "Peace offering, or repentance for yesterday's shenanigans?"

Her eyes crinkled at the corners when she laughed, making her look adorable. "Both." She lifted an eyebrow, just a little. "But yes, peace offering. Because you were also mean, Branson Black."

He chuckled, the sound unfamiliar to him, and he fought to take it back but it was too late. Her grin widened.

"Mean?"

"Yes," she asserted firmly. "Mean. So I brought you some things to maybe help with that."

He looked in the bag. He could see a bottle of wine, a few packages of snacks, a pound of coffee and a mug. "What's all this?"

With a pleased expression, she said, "I figured you're either stressed and need a drink, are grouchy from hunger, or undercaffeinated." She hesitated, then added, "Yesterday notwithstanding. That was terrible judgment on my part, and I'm sorry."

He was charmed. He couldn't help it. Particularly because she was blunt and right. He had been mean. And yesterday she had shown terrible judgment.

"You're still after my lighthouse."

She sobered. "There are no strings attached to this gift. I didn't listen to you, and yesterday I acted impulsively. I could have been in danger, and you went to great trouble to make sure I was okay. This really is just a thank you."

He didn't want to like her, but he did. She was so upfront. And she didn't tiptoe around him, like anyone else who knew who he really was. He stepped back and opened the door wider, a silent invitation. He didn't always have to be rude. And she'd apologized, which he appreciated.

Truthfully, his ogre status was getting hard to maintain. It wasn't his normal way. It was just his way of punishing himself.

She stepped inside and halted in the foyer. "Now that's something. I didn't have a chance to tell you yesterday, but this—" she swept her arm out wide "—this makes a statement."

A table sat in the middle of the open space, while the hardwood staircase wound around it, forming a column that went to the top of the house. A skylight there beamed sunlight into the entry, a natural spotlight on the flower arrangement on the pedestal table.

"It does give some wow factor," Bran admitted.

"It sure does. This is a gorgeous place. Airy and roomy."

"Since you've only been three feet inside the foyer, would you like the twenty-five-cent tour?"

Did he really just say that?

"Sure. I promise to keep my camera in my tote bag this time."

He looked over, and her face held an impish expression that made his lips twitch. "Ha ha. Come on. I'll put this in the kitchen first."

He led her through the expansive downstairs. The kitchen was spacious and modern, and while he'd furnished one of the large living rooms, he'd left the other, the one closer to the den, unfurnished. She made appropriate sounds of approval at his den, and then they went upstairs, where she gave a cursory glance at the bedrooms and then sighed at the ensuite bath, which had a stunning view of the water. "Oh, man," she murmured, stepping inside. "A Jacuzzi tub with an ocean view. All you'd need is a book and a glass of wine and you'd be in heaven."

He was treated to a vision of what that might look like; her pale skin surrounded by bubbles and damp tendrils of hair down her neck...a long, wet leg and flushed cheeks from the heat of the bath. He tried, unsuccessfully, to shake the image from his mind. A better idea would be to get her out of his house. Or at least out of the upstairs.

She turned to him then and put a hand on his arm. "I have a confession to make. I figured out who you were after my first visit here. Now I kind of understand why you were so angry. I know I violated your privacy. I really did just come to say that I'm sorry. For everything, Mr. Black."

He hated being called Mr. Black. It reminded him of his father, who had insisted on it from nearly everyone. The only person he'd ever heard call him Peter was his mother. And it had always been Peter, and never Pete. "Branson," he replied, taken aback by her honest little speech. "And I was rude. You're right. I didn't have to be such an ass."

She laughed. "Thanks for the tour, but I should probably get going."

She slid by him, trailing a scent of something that reminded him of lily of the valley.

It really had been a peace offering, then. She hadn't pressed her case about the lighthouse. Hadn't asked him a thing about his books or his family…and what happened was no secret. It had been all over the internet and made it to several print publications. The one good thing about being an author was that his face was less recognizable than other celebrities. Clearly it hadn't escaped her notice, though.

Then again, she was somewhat of a celebrity herself, at least in the art world. Or so it would seem.

"Miss Blundon?"

She turned around and smiled. "If I have to call you Branson, you have to call me Jess."

"Jess." It suited her. "About yesterday… I own part of the blame. If I hadn't been such a jerk, you wouldn't have had to rent a boat. What I'm saying is…if you want to take some pics of the lighthouse, that would be okay."

The way her face lit up made him glad he'd said it. Her eyes sparkled, and her smile was wide and free and full of joy. How long had it been since he'd felt such an unfettered, positive emotion?

Not even at Jeremy and Tori's wedding had he felt so light. Their wedding had been a happy, wonderful occasion, but bittersweet for Bran. He'd been remembering his own wedding day years earlier.

But this was simpler. Granting a small favor, really, and it felt good.

"Really? I'd love that! Would it be possible to do a few sketches while I'm here?"

How could he say no now? Suddenly he realized he'd put himself in an awkward position. He'd thought a few pictures wouldn't hurt. But he wasn't sure he wanted her hanging around.

Her smile faded, and she put a hand on his arm. "I'm sorry. If it's too much, just say so."

The warmth of her hand seeped into his skin. Her fingers were strong, elegant and slim, like a pianist's, and unadorned with any rings or nail polish. Was he enjoying the contact a little too much?

"A few sketches would be okay," he answered, then cleared his throat. "I won't jump down your throat if I see you at the lighthouse, okay?"

She squeezed his arm. "You mean I have permission to access it?"

He had no idea why he was going along with this, other than the fact that he knew he'd been horribly grouchy the day before, and he didn't like that about himself. "Yes, that's what I mean."

Her gaze softened. "Thank you," she said quietly. "I've had such a hard time lately, and this is the first place that's really fired up my creativity. It means more than you know."

He could relate. He hadn't written a word in nearly two years. But he merely nodded as she turned away and started down the stairs. He followed closely behind, not too closely, though. And wondered at the strange feeling settling in the middle of his chest. It was pleasure mixed with anxiety, an odd combination of enjoying the contact while feeling like it was a foreign sensation.

Had he been hiding away too long?

He walked her to the door, feeling more unsure of himself with each step. When they reached the threshold, she opened the door and stepped outside, then turned around to face him.

"I know this probably sounds presumptuous and odd, but do you think we could be friends?"

He chuckled dryly. "That is not what I expected you to say."

She shrugged. "Just to clear the air, I read the news. I'm very sorry for your loss, and I understand that it takes time to recover from something like that. I lost someone very special to me around the same time."

He swallowed around the lump that had suddenly appeared in his throat. "Thank you."

"And I just started painting again. So just so you know, giving me access to the lighthouse actually means a lot. There were times I thought I'd never feel that passion again, but here I am." She spread her arms wide.

She didn't say that he'd get there too. Didn't

give assurances that all he needed was time. Simply said that it meant a lot to her. He appreciated that more than she could know. He'd just about had it with the well-meaning but empty platitudes.

"You're welcome," he replied, his voice rough.

There was a pause while he searched for the right way to say goodbye. She shifted her weight to her other hip and then smiled again. "Okay, so I'd better go. Have a good day, Branson."

"You too. And thank you for the peace offering." He attempted to smile back and saw her eyes widen. Wow. Did he really smile so rarely that it came as a complete surprise?

"Okay…bye, then." She took a step backward, then gave a little wave before turning away from him and heading across the lawn toward the bluff and the red-and-white sentinel standing guard.

He shut the door, then went to his den. The broad expanse of windows gave him a perfect view, and he watched as she picked her way over rocks and bumps, her footsteps sure and light. She pulled out her camera and started snapping, and after a while put it away and pulled out a sketch pad. A half smile on his face, he shook his head as she picked a large rock for a seat, plopped herself on it and started to draw.

Then he sat down and opened his laptop. Stared at the screen for a few minutes, then opened his browser.

He wasn't quite ready. But for the first time since losing Jennie and Owen, he felt that someday he might be.

Jess hadn't planned to stay at the Sandpiper so long, and when Tori offered up her boathouse as an alternative place to stay, Jess snapped it up immediately. The building was adorable, with a warm and welcoming red door, tons of natural light, the coziest of galley kitchens and a single bedroom. The bunk beds inside had a small double on the bottom and a single on the top, so she put her clothes in the tiny dresser and made herself comfortable on the mattress with the cheery comforter sporting nautical designs in navy, red and white.

According to Tori, she and Jeremy had considered making it a vacation rental. But they were waiting to do that since Tori's time was taken up with being a brand-new mom. Jess stared up at the bottom of the bunk above her and let out a happy sigh. She'd take this over a hotel room any day.

After a twenty-minute nap, she got up and

went to the kitchen to make a cup of tea. While it was steeping, she looked around the tiny living room and examined the light sources. Sketching wasn't a big deal. If she wanted to paint, she had different requirements for light and space. A few adjustments and she'd moved some of the furniture, pushing it closer to the wall. The wicker rocking chair found a new home on the sweet white-railed porch, and she wondered if Tori would be amenable to taking out the coffee table altogether. Then it would be just about right.

But she wasn't ready to start painting yet. Today she'd started some preliminary sketches that she liked but wasn't crazy over. Carrying her tea, sketch pad and pencils, she went to the porch and sat in the afternoon sun, sipping and contemplating. She turned the page over and started something different. Just the very edge of the lighthouse intruded on the right-hand side of the paper; and then, just to the left of center, she started moving her pencil, beginning an outline of a man, hands in his pockets, staring out to sea.

There was something captivating about him. She wanted to say that it wasn't because of his celebrity, but now that she knew, it kind of was. She'd read one or two of his books...figured he'd released something like ten now, maybe a dozen. Mysteries and procedurals, where she couldn't wait to turn another page and was afraid to at the same time. She admired a brain like that, so willing to wander into the darkness and face it unflinchingly, and with such detail. Now, having met him, and knowing he was grieving, she had another impression. In all his books, there was still a thread of hope through them. The bad guy always got what was coming to him. The main characters always came through with a happy ending.

He didn't get his happy ending, though. She knew how that felt. Broken hearts, crushed dreams. Jess had never quite had the family she'd always wanted. And as she made sweep after sweep on her pad, she saw the outline of a broken man coming through.

She didn't notice the time until the sun went behind the trees, dimming her light. She'd been working for hours, and she tilted her neck, working out a creak. With a sigh she picked up her phone and checked her messages. There was one from Tori, inviting her up for drinks later. She checked the time…inviting her for drinks in twenty minutes, to be exact. She'd worked throughout the late afternoon and what normally would have been dinner. She went inside, closing the red door behind her, and opened the fridge. She wasn't about to have drinks on an empty stomach, so she took out a container of hummus and nibbled on some crackers and veggies. Her hair was tucked in a bun and held there with a pencil, but she didn't really care. It was Tori and Jeremy, and they seemed like the most laid back people she'd ever met. On went her flat sandals, a quick smooth over her flowy skirt, and she was off along the gravel path to the main house.

Branson's car was in the driveway and she hesitated, wondering if Tori had asked him to join them. They'd made peace yesterday, but she wasn't sure she was ready for couples drinks and a social call where he was concerned. She nearly turned back when Tori's voice called her name. She couldn't turn around now and pretend she hadn't heard. Her careless hair and slightly wrinkled skirt would have to do. And she could fake her way through small talk, couldn't she?

"Hi!" she called out, skirting the house and heading to the backyard patio. Clearly this was where the action was in the Fisher house. She shivered; it was only May, and she hadn't thought to bring a sweater.

"Hi yourself," Tori offered. "I'm out here grabbing Rose's blanket. I left it out earlier. Come on inside."

Grateful to be going inside for the visit, Jess

let out a breath and held the door as Tori went in, her arms full of baby and blanket. Jeremy was at the island pouring drinks. "Hey, Jess," he said. "Glad you could come up."

"Jess?"

She turned around abruptly. Bran was there, at the end of the hall, staring at her. Oh, Lord. He hadn't known she was invited. Her face heated and then together they stared at Tori, whose eyebrows lifted in an expression of innocence.

"What? Jess is staying in our boathouse so she can paint. And you haven't been over in a week. What's the big deal?"

Bran leveled his gaze on her. "Because you set it up, Miss Innocent."

Great. He had no desire to be there with her. And she wasn't exactly comfortable, but she wouldn't have put it precisely that way. Then again, her initial encounters with Branson had demonstrated his usual manner was blunt.

Jess stared at both of them, then over at Jeremy, who cracked open a can of tonic water. "Don't look at me," he said, pouring the fizzy liquid into a glass.

Tori kept the innocent look on her face. "What? You guys can be civil, right? Lord, it's not like I set you up on a blind date or something."

Except it felt like it. Jeremy pressed a glass of merlot into her hands with a murmur of, "Humor her." The glass of tonic and lime went to Tori. "Bran?" he asked. "What are you having?"

"That tonic will be fine. I'm driving, after all."

Huh. That was surprising. She admired his zero tolerance attitude. "I'm lucky I just have to walk down the path," she said, trying to lighten the awkward atmosphere. "The boathouse is perfect, Tori. I was wondering though if there's somewhere I could put the coffee table? The living room is perfect for me to work."

"Of course!" Tori sat on the sofa and Jess sat beside her, and they immediately started chatting about the boathouse, the decorations and Jess's future plans for it. It was a good distraction from glancing at Bran the whole time, who was still looking rather hermit-like, but with a pressed shirt and his hair tucked behind his ears. The first time they'd met, she'd thought him to be in his forties, but now she thought it was probably younger. Midthirties, maybe. She tried to imagine him with a man bun and nearly laughed out loud. That wasn't for Bran.

He was too... She frowned. *Too much* was all she could seem to come up with. Jeremy said something and Bran chuckled, a low, rough vibration that reached in and ignited something in her belly. Oh, no. This was not a good thing. He was far easier to dismiss as a grouchy old ogre. She didn't actually want to like him. Or feel the stirrings of, if not attraction, curiosity. She was after his lighthouse. Nothing more. Even if she had started to sketch him earlier today.

Jeremy got up and refilled her wineglass and she settled back down into the sofa, relaxing more. She had friends, of course she did. But over the last few days she had thought back to those relationships. Some were lifers. Some had been relationships of utility, for a time only and then moving on or drifting apart. Some had been intense and brief, leaving her an empty vessel at the end. She listened to Jeremy and Branson and heard that rusty laugh again... They had been friends since they were boys. Jeremy drew her and Tori into the conversation with tales from Merrick Hall, the prep school he and Bran had attended together. Before long they were laughing, and Jessica was wondering about the third best friend, Cole, who sounded like the instigator of the bunch. How wonderful it must be to have friends like that. Like she'd been with Ana. There were times she just missed her so much.

She was just lifting her glass to take a sip when Bran's gaze reached over and held hers.

Unlike their other meetings, this time his eyes were warm and hypnotizing, his lips holding the tiniest bit of humor, slightly hidden by his beard. Her body responded; there was something untamed about him that drew her in. Which sounded silly, of course. He was anything but uncivilized. Perhaps it was just his restless energy. Whatever it was, she couldn't look away.

Tori appeared with some crudités and crackers, and Jess averted her eyes and instead focused on fixing a cracker with soft cheese and red pepper jelly. It was delicious, and since she'd missed having a real meal at dinnertime, a welcome addition to her stomach after two glasses of wine. When baby Rose woke and needed attending, Jess felt it was time to make her excuses and head home. Tori would be wanting to settle the baby and get some rest.

Bran seemed to agree, because he stood and collected glasses from the coffee table. "Thanks for having me over," he said, taking them to the kitchen.

"It's good for the hermit to come out of his cave once in a while."

Jess couldn't help it. She snorted as she carried dirty plates to the sink. Tori grinned and Jeremy gave Bran a slap on the back.

"Hey, I get out." Bran aimed a sharp look

at Jess, a teasing glint in his eye. "I mean two days ago is a prime example."

"Branson," she said firmly, wishing he wouldn't tell this story. But Tori and Jeremy were staring at them both, and Branson smiled. She really wished he wouldn't do that. His smile was devastating.

"What happened?" Jeremy took the bait.

Jess attempted a preemptive strike. "Branson gave me a lift to the resort from the boat rental place, that's all." She pinned Bran with a "please don't do it" glare.

"What were you doing at the boat rental place?"

"I'd rented a boat."

"But what was Bran doing there?"

He lifted his eyebrows and grinned again. "Come on, Jessica. It's a good story."

"It's embarrassing."

"Hey, you laughed at the story about my underwear earlier. Fair's fair."

He was right. She'd giggled at the antics of the boys at boarding school, while sympathizing with the children they'd been, finding love and acceptance among strangers rather than at home. She was going to say he'd been thirteen at the time, but she also knew Tori was not going to let them leave without him spilling the beans. She sighed and capitulated. "Fine."

She shouldn't have worried. It became crystal clear that Bran was a born storyteller. Tori rocked Rose in her arms and Jeremy stopped putting dishes in the dishwasher as Bran told the tale with suspense in all the right spots, a dash of humor here and there, and without making her sound utterly stupid. Even she was caught up in it, and she was the subject! He finished with, "So I gave her the car and I took the boat back to Cummins's, and then dropped her off at the resort."

Tori shook her head. "What an adventure!"

Jess folded her hands. "Well, all's well that ends well. Rather than see me risk my own neck again, Branson let me take some pictures of the lighthouse, so I don't anticipate any new nautical mishaps for a good long while."

"You brought me food. What was I going to say?"

She laughed. "You could have kicked me off your property like you did the first day. Or ignore me altogether."

"Ignoring you would only have made you do something crazier."

She suddenly realized that Jeremy and Tori were watching them with amused expressions. "And on that note, I think it's time I headed to the boathouse. Thank you both for inviting me up."

"Don't be silly. We're friends now. You can stay in the boathouse as long as you need. You can be our vacation rental trial run. And the door is always open. It's nice having you around."

"I'd better head out too," Bran said. "New parents need their sleep."

He said it easily, but Jess caught a glimpse of something on his face, a tension around his mouth that hadn't been there before. He and Jeremy were best friends. It had to be a painful reminder to see his friend happily married with a new baby, when Bran had had those things and lost them.

"I'll be in touch about the property for Cole," Jeremy said, oblivious to Bran's expression. "You can help me with that if you like. Something new just came on the market that might be perfect."

"Sounds good," Bran said.

He followed Jess to the front door, and they waved goodbye to their hosts. She expected him to head to his car while she took the path to the boathouse, but he fell into step beside her.

"What are you doing?"

"Walking you home."

She sighed. "It's not necessary. I'm not in danger of capsizing on my way to the boathouse."

"No, but you also didn't turn a light on."

Darn, he was right. The boathouse loomed in the darkness, and she could make out the form of the porch, but she hadn't turned on the outside light.

"The light attracts bugs," she explained.

He chuckled. She wished he would stop doing that. It made her insides all warm and tingly.

Their feet made soft crunching noises on the graveled path. Jess could hear the sound of the ocean shushing against the sand, and somewhere nearby, in a tall tree, an owl hooted. She sighed, loving the solitude and peace of this place. "That's a great horned owl," she said softly. "Who cooks for you?"

"What?"

"Listen to his call. *Who cooks for you?*"

The owl hooted again, and Bran murmured, "Well, I'll be damned."

She smiled in the darkness. It took only another few moments and they were at the porch of the boathouse. "I didn't lock the door," she said, "so I don't need to see the lock. Thank you for walking me, though."

"You're welcome."

"Branson?"

It sounded odd, using his first name, but after yesterday's rescue, it hardly seemed necessary to call him Mr. Black.

"Yes?"

His voice was husky in the dark. She held in a sigh.

"You are a wonderful storyteller. I was so afraid you were going to throw me under the bus in there. But you didn't. You made it sound like some great adventure. Even I was waiting to hear what happened next, and I was there."

"Thanks."

She put her hand on his arm. It was firm and warm beneath her fingers. "What I'm trying to say is…don't give up."

Silence fell between them for a few moments, and Jess found herself looking into his dark gaze. The shadows only lent to the intimacy of the moment, and briefly she wondered if he were going to kiss her.

But then the moment seemed to pass, and she took her hand off his arm. She'd said enough, and hopefully had given him something to think about. "Good night," she whispered, then went inside and shut the door.

CHAPTER FOUR

FOR THREE DAYS Branson watched as Jessica sketched at the lighthouse. After the first day, he left the gate open so she wouldn't have to walk so far. He'd spent his time doing some research. Not for a book, but on the lighthouse he now owned. He wanted to know more about the history of it, and so he'd dug into Google, visited the local library and accessed the provincial archives. The lighthouse was over a century old, made defunct after World War II, and most importantly, he'd found a book from the seventies with ghost stories and local lore at the library that he found most intriguing. His lighthouse had a history, with enough mystery to have his mind turning a plot over and over in his mind.

"You are a wonderful storyteller," she'd said. The compliment had taken him by surprise. He wasn't even sure why he'd felt compelled to recount the incident at all; maybe to prove

to Jeremy that he wasn't the hermit everyone said he was. Maybe because he'd missed it. Or maybe just because he'd enjoyed the evening so much, and seeing the gleam in Jessica's eyes.

Her eyes were rather extraordinary.

He took his glass of iced water upstairs and went out on the balcony. He could see the point so clearly here, and Jess had started bringing a folding chair rather than perching on a rock to do her sketching. He'd been watching her for a few hours now, wondering if she'd put sunscreen on her fair skin; the spring sun was still capable of delivering a sunburn even though the temperatures were cool, particularly near the water. After a while he wondered if she'd eaten anything all day. He certainly hadn't seen her put her work aside to break for lunch. Did she get a crick in her neck sitting like that, as he did when he sat at his computer too long?

And why was he standing here thinking of all these questions?

It was going on two when he emerged from the house carrying a plastic bag in lieu of any sort of picnic basket. The wind buffeted his shirt and the chill reached inside him, even as the sun warmed the top of his head. Jessica didn't hear him approach until he was a handful of steps away from her, then she looked up and a smile lit her face. It had been an unconscious response, he realized, and the idea that she'd been glad to see him sent a spiral of warmth through his body.

It was only some lunch. Nothing major. He didn't need to feel…guilty. They were friends. Maybe not even friends. More like *friendly*.

"Hi," she greeted, putting down her pencil. "What brings you out here?"

He lifted his hand. "Food. I don't think you've eaten, and the last thing I need is you fainting and falling off a cliff and me having to rescue you again."

She laughed, that light, easy sound he'd enjoyed the other night, too. He even smiled a little in response.

"I promise I would not faint. Or fall off a cliff. I'm made of tough stuff. But I am hungry. What time is it?"

"Nearly two."

"Oh, my." She stretched her neck, first lifting her face to the sky, then leaning it toward her right shoulder. "I had no idea."

Bran lifted the bag. "It's not much, but I thought you could use a bite."

"That's very kind of you."

He handed her the bag and then moved away, turning to face the house again.

"Aren't you going to join me?"

He shouldn't want to. That he did—very

much—was exactly why he shouldn't. He turned back to face her and hesitated, long enough for her to nod at the flat rock nearby. "There's room for both of us there, and I'll share."

A part of him said, *What would it hurt?* while a second part reminded him that Jennie and Owen would never again have picnics on a cliff on a spring day.

Jessica got up from her seat and tucked her sketch pad and pencils away in her bag, then grabbed the lunch bag and went to his side. "You have that hermit look on your face again. What is it?"

"I shouldn't be here."

"Why?"

She asked the simplest and hardest questions. Then she reached down and took his hand. "Is it because it feels too much like living again?"

He pulled his hand away. "Stop it. Stop trying to get into my head."

She didn't get upset. Didn't get mad or sad or indignant. That might have been easier. Instead, she just looked at him, her face open and honest and dammit, compassionate. "I'm sorry." Her voice was quiet and sincere. "You have to get through this on your own time. Thank you for the lunch. It's very thoughtful."

He started walking back to the house. Got about fifty feet and turned back, his stomach churning. She was sitting on the rock, peering inside the bag and looking lonely. He'd snapped at her when she hadn't deserved it. "Yes," he called out, and she lifted her head. "Yes, because of that."

Jessica nodded, then shifted over and patted the rock beside her. "The invitation is still open, and I'll mind my own business."

He doubted that. And the odd thing about it was that he wasn't sure he wanted her to. There were so many feelings bubbling inside him, feelings he hadn't been able to share with his family, or even with Jeremy and Cole. He could just imagine the looks on their faces if he shared his deepest thoughts. Those thoughts were pretty dark. But how long could he hold them inside?

Slowly, he made his way back to her and sat on the rock, resting his elbows on his knees. "Here," she said, taking half the chicken sandwich he'd made and handing it to him. "Eat half. There's too much in here for me anyway."

He took the sandwich and took a bite. She did the same, and after she chewed and swallowed, she lifted her face to the sun again, drinking it in. He stared at the column of her neck and had trouble swallowing his bite of sandwich.

When she lowered her chin, he took another bite and moved his focus to the sea spread out before them. True to her word, she didn't say anything. Just ate the lunch he'd prepared—the sandwich, some sliced apples and a couple of cookies he'd had in the pantry—and drank the water bottle full of lemonade he'd put inside.

She took a drink and then offered it to him. He accepted, took a long pull of the sweet and tart liquid, and then handed it back.

"Your lemonade is very good." She smiled as she offered the compliment, and then bit into a chocolate chip cookie.

"Thanks."

She grinned. "After your stories last night, I kind of thought you might have servants to help with things like picnic packing."

Bran angled her a sideways glance, and realized she was attempting to lighten the mood by teasing him. "Oh, my parents still do. The perks of an affluent childhood—never having to lift a finger."

"Or have the satisfaction of accomplishment?"

His lips dropped open in surprise. "Yes, I suppose." He pondered for a moment. "I guess that's the difference between entitlement and actual achievement, isn't it?"

"There's something rewarding about self-sufficiency."

Jess's lips set in a line as she said it. He wanted to ask her what she meant, but was afraid of either of them prying too deeply into past issues. Instead, he turned to the topic at hand, and gestured toward her bag with her sketching materials.

"Your drawings are coming along okay?"

She nodded. "I'm having so much fun. It's a combination of things, I think. The location is simply amazing. But I also think I finally got to a place mentally where I am ready to create again. It feels like the magic happens from both things coming together at the same time. Just the sketching is giving me so much joy."

He hesitated for a long moment, then said, "Do you ever feel guilty for being happy?" He couldn't look at her, but he felt her gaze on him. Nerves churned in his belly just asking the question. Not that he was happy. He wasn't. But could he go through his whole life like this? Did he want to?

"You mean do I feel guilty moving on after grieving someone so close to me?"

He nodded, unable to speak. It seemed they were going to get into the difficult subjects anyway.

"Not now. But I did for a long time. I felt as if I didn't deserve to be happy. That I somehow owed it to Ana to be miserable. And so I was." After a pause she added, "It's a hell of a way to live. I did the same after my mother died, though it was different. My parents divorced when I was ten. I guess I just… I don't know. Didn't feel as emotionally safe with my family as I did with my best friend. She'd never given me a reason to doubt. Besides, I think we grieve different people in different ways."

Another few moments of silence, and then she spoke again. "And I didn't lose my spouse and my child. I can't know what you're going through, Branson. I just know that someday you should be happy again, and not feel as if you're betraying them by moving on."

Tears stung the back of his eyes. She had spoken in a plain manner, with truth and gentleness, and said words that not even his best friends could manage. They tried to bring him back to the world of the living, but they didn't talk about the grief. It was painful relief to be able to do so.

"It's been two years. Owen would have been three now. We might have had more children. And I can't remember…" He swallowed heavily, fighting tears. "I can't remember the exact sound of his voice when he said *Dada*. Why can't I remember that?"

He didn't realize he was actually crying until Jessica put the bag aside and shuffled over, putting her arms around him. Then he noticed the wetness in his beard and on his cheeks. He was mortified to be falling apart in front of her, but he was helpless to stop it.

"It's okay," she said, rubbing his back. "Every single thing you feel and say is okay. There is no one way to grieve and no timetable."

He sniffed and rubbed his hands over his face. "I'm so sorry. A week ago I was yelling at you and now I'm bawling all over you."

"Don't apologize. I get it. It's probably easier with someone you don't know." Her hand still made circles on his back, and it felt warm and reassuring. He'd been so touch starved. He should move away, but he wasn't ready to yet. She rested the crest of her cheek on his shoulder for a moment. "When Ana died, it was like all the light went out of everything. She was my rock and my best friend. She'd seen me through creative slumps and successes. Through relationships that came and went…she was my person. When I lost her, I lost my anchor and my compass all at once. But eventually I realized that she would be so angry with me for not living.

"It wasn't like flipping a switch, you know? It wasn't like I decided to live again and just started doing it. I had to take baby steps. I stumbled a lot. I pushed through when joy was just not showing up. But happiness is a little like creative inspiration. Sometimes we can't sit around and wait for it to show up. Sometimes we need to go looking for it. Or at least put ourselves out there so we can grab pieces of it when it rushes by."

"I don't know how to do that."

"You will. Something will snag in your brain, and you'll feel the urge to write it down. Or little snippets will come to you, and you'll write a bit and hate it, maybe, but little by little it'll happen. And when it does, you mustn't feel guilty about it."

"Is that how it's been for you?"

She nodded against his shoulder. "At first I started little random sketches. Then I thought I'd travel around and try to get back in the groove again. This past week, here? I finally feel energized and excited to work on something. And I know Ana would want me to."

"What happened to her?"

Jessica paused, then sighed, a sorrowful sound that made him want to hug her back. "She had cancer. One day she was fine. The next day she had stage four pancreatic cancer. In less than three months she was gone."

He could hear the grief in her voice, and he reached over and put his hand over hers. "I'm sorry."

"Thank you."

They sat, comfortable with quiet, for a few minutes. Then Jessica leaned away, taking her arms from around him, letting out a sigh. "It really is beautiful here. So wild and untamed."

Gulls swooped overhead, and Bran let the sun soak into his skin as the dull roar of the ocean on the rocks below filled his ears. "It can be lonely," he admitted. "And comforting at the same time."

"I get that," she agreed. She looked over at him. "You okay now?"

He nodded. "I am. Sorry I got all emotional."

"You don't have to apologize to me," she replied. Then she smiled. "Though I do think this qualifies us as actual friends now."

His gaze dropped to her lips. He shouldn't be thinking it, but he wasn't sure she was the kind of woman he could ever be just friends with. It was probably good she was just here for a short time.

"Friends," he echoed. "You're sure?"

"You brought me lunch. We shared stuff. Pretty sure that makes us friends." She leaned back onto her arms. He smiled as he looked over at her. She was so artless. Now she was sunning herself like a lizard on a rock. He did like her. Very much.

"Well, then," he answered, and adopted a similar posture.

They sat for several minutes, until the sun went under a cloud and the wind took on a chilly bite. "I should probably pack up for the day," Jessica said on a sigh. "I'm going to lose the best light."

"How much longer are you staying on the South Shore?"

She shrugged. "I don't know. A month? Two? Tori and Jeremy have said I can rent the boathouse for as long as I need. I'm going to start painting soon."

There was a hesitation in her voice that told him maybe she wasn't quite ready yet, but he wasn't going to call her on it. As she said, it took baby steps. If she was finding joy, he was happy for her.

And maybe one day he'd find joy, too.

Jessica pressed the cell phone to her ear and let out a sigh. "I know, Jack. I know. It's been a long time. But I don't want this to be rushed. For God's sake, I haven't even started the actual paintings."

His voice was sharp and clear. "Sure, but you're excited. I can tell. And we can set up a showing now for fall. I just need the commitment from you."

She pinched the top of her nose with two fingers. "That's too fast. The fact that I'm even working again is a blessing. I don't want to add the pressure of a show when I might only get one decent painting from this summer. I'm sorry Jack, but the answer's no."

He softened his voice. "Hey, I know you're scared. Coming back is hard. The world just needs more Jessica Blundon art. You're going to be back in Chicago by the fall, right?"

"I was planning on it. I can stay here for a few months, but I do have to go home sometime."

"Then let me do some asking around. We might be able to work something really innovative without booking an actual show. An exclusive, a handful of paintings maybe. Tie it in with something else. Just say you'll stay open to possibilities."

She laughed a little. "I always stay open to possibilities. And you are too coercive for your own good, Jack."

"Which is why I'm your best agent." Affection and teasing came over the line, and she relaxed a bit. "I don't want to stifle your creativity with pressure, but I also don't want you to miss out on opportunities. I'll be in touch."

"All right."

"Love you, kiddo."

Her eyes stung a little from the easy declaration. "I love you too, Jack. Thanks for not bailing on me."

"Never. Chat soon."

She hung up the call and sighed. The idea of having a showing in the autumn was exciting, but she was sure she wouldn't be ready. While she was ready to work, and even enthusiastic, there was no guarantee that every single work would be ready to show. For now she wanted to create and just revel in the process again. Feel the brush in her hand, the pressure of the bristles on canvas like a beautiful, private language only she could understand. The colors and the smell of paint and turpentine, acrid and as much a scent of home to her as bread baking or apple pie. The scrape of the palette knife. The process was the essence of who she was. She didn't care about shows or accolades. Right now feeling like herself again was all she wanted to focus on.

The rest would come. In time.

She was late getting to the lighthouse because of Jack's call, and the wind was particularly brutal, whipping her hair out of its braid and lifting the corners of her sketch pad. She clipped them down and tried to ignore the gusts that slapped at her, instead focusing on the door of the lighthouse. It was beautifully scarred, the rusty hinges crooked but strong enough that the door didn't droop. It looked as if it hadn't been used in ages, maybe decades, and the battered boards seemed almost like a fingerprint of what time had wrought.

At the foot of the door, just to the side, was a small clump of daisies, stubbornly blooming against the elements and in the rocky soil. Jessica dashed her pencil across the paper, capturing their proud, resilient heads. She smiled, and wrote along the bottom right corner, *Marguerite*. It was the French word for *daisy*, and it felt right.

"Good afternoon."

She jumped, grateful that her soft pencil hadn't been against paper. Bran stood just beside her and behind, his hands in his pockets. "Sorry," he said. "I didn't mean to scare you."

"It's so windy I didn't hear you." She rolled her shoulders. "I've been admiring the daisies. Pretty stubborn to be blooming amid all this salt and rock."

He looked over her shoulder at her sketch. "You like the door."

"It has character. And secrets."

To her surprise, a smile spread across his face. "Are you interested in finding out what some of those secrets are?"

"What do you mean?"

He took a key from his pocket. It was big and old, and she wondered if it would still work. "It works," he said, as if reading her mind. "I had the building inspected before I closed the purchase. The structure is old, but it's sturdy."

Excitement bloomed in her chest. "Of course I want to see inside!" She gave him some side-eye. "Unless it's overrun with mice. In which case I'm not too keen."

"Fair enough. And I haven't been inside either, by the way. First sign of rodents, we're out."

She stood up and tucked her sketch pad away. "Are you kidding? You haven't gone in, not once? You've been here since…"

"February," he supplied. "And it is damned cold here in February. Now though… I'm curious. I thought you might be, too."

"I am. I've never been inside an actual lighthouse before."

This one was small compared to many, but she was interested to see what surprises and treasures were inside. Bran went to the door and fiddled for a while, jiggling the key in the lock. "I wonder if the salt rusted the lock?" he mused, but then the key seemed to find home and turned over with a solid click.

The hinges creaked as he pushed the door open.

She followed behind, stepping into the hollow-sounding space that closed out the sound of the wind. The bottom of the lighthouse was simply a large, single room. An old army cot was against one wall, with a wool blanket heavy with dust covering the mattress. There was a table and chairs there, too, and an oil lantern—empty—sitting on the table. A space jutted out from the otherwise square base of the lighthouse, and a wood stove was in the corner, the flue vented out through the top of the addition. When Bran went to examine it, she stopped him. "Don't," she said quickly. "I promise I'm not usually a wimp, but I have visions of that stove either being full of mice or that birds have made a nest in there."

He chuckled and stepped back. "I'll explore that on my own, then."

"Thank you." She shuddered. She hated mice, and she also hated the thought of a bird flying out of the iron stove and getting trapped in the room.

"It's pretty plain, isn't it?"

She wandered over to the army cot, pushed

up against the wall. What a lonely spot. "Was there ever a lighthouse keeper?"

He nodded. "The lighthouse was made defunct in the late forties, after the war. But before that there was. And one before him. Back to 1893, when the lighthouse was built. There was a house, too, but it burned in the twenties, apparently."

She was intrigued. The light in the room was dark and gloomy, thanks to a lack of windows. A sparse amount of sunshine traveled down to the bottom level from a singular window above, along the staircase that led to the actual lamp. She went to the staircase and looked over at him. "I'm lighter. I'll go first and make sure it's sound."

"Please be careful."

She smiled in reply and turned her attention to the rough steps leading to the top. The spiral staircase was narrow, but solid, and Jessica held on to the handrail as she climbed up…and up…and up, Branson's footsteps close behind. She reached a trapdoor at the top, and with a little help from Branson, released the closure and pushed it open.

Light poured in, brash and cheery, along with a gust of cool air. Apparently the windows at the top were not airtight, and the wind gusted around the structure, whistling eerily through the cracks.

Jessica had never been a big fan of heights, but she couldn't deny the view was spectacular. She could see for miles—up and down the coast, and also inland, to where the main road cut through the trees and clearings where other houses were built. None of them were as grand as Bran's.

"Wow," Branson said, standing close behind her. There wasn't much room in the top, and she could feel the warmth of his body near her back. "It's tiny. But look at the size of the lamp."

She looked. "I can't even see a bulb or anything. Is there one?"

"I think it's so old it might have been a lantern. And all these lenses. Cool, right?"

It was cool. It was one of the neatest things she'd ever seen. And the lenses...so many angles and slivers of light and texture. She wished she'd brought her camera. Wondered if Bran would let her come in here again. She thought about the challenge of painting simply *light*. Tingles ran down her arms and she turned to him. "I need to paint this. Look. It's all glass and angles and light and can you imagine what it would look like on canvas?"

His gaze locked with hers, and the power of

it slammed into her. They were utterly alone, at the top of an abandoned lighthouse, and the intimacy of the moment was too strong to be ignored. His gaze dropped to her lips briefly, and a slow burn ignited low in her pelvis…attraction. Desire. She tried to push it away. She had no business being attracted to him, especially after their rather personal conversation earlier in the week. He certainly wasn't in any headspace to return any attraction.

"Do you want to go outside?" His voice was rough as he backed away and moved toward a small door leading to the 360-degree platform.

She inhaled a deep breath and accepted the distraction gratefully. "Yes, but I don't trust that railing."

"Me either. It's probably rotted. Stay close to the building."

She followed him out, watched as he gingerly stepped on the platform. Despite its age, the wood seemed mostly sound. She stayed close to the wall, buffeted by the wind until they reached the other side of the lighthouse, which was sheltered and afforded a view that went miles down the coast. The water sparkled so brightly it hurt her eyes, but her chest filled with the fresh, salty air, and she felt a freedom she hadn't felt in a long, long time.

She turned and saw Bran watching her, and

she smiled, feeling a connection with him that was new. He smiled back, surprising her, and stepped closer. Her heart hammered at his nearness. A pair of gulls screeched, their cries swallowed by a gust of wind.

"Bran," she murmured.

His gaze tangled with hers, dark, complicated. She shouldn't want him to be nearer. Should suggest they go back inside. Should say she was cold or something…but the truth was she wasn't cold and she didn't want to go back inside and she wanted to sink her hands into his rich mane of hair and feel his beard against the soft skin of her face. Oh, Lord. They had just said they were friends. Now she wasn't so sure.

And she'd called him by a shortened version of his name. Not Branson, but Bran. It seemed too intimate and yet suited him perfectly.

"Jess," he answered, also shortening her name, and all the delicious tension ratcheted up a notch.

He lifted his hand, cupped the back of her head and drew her close. She had barely caught her breath when he dropped his mouth to hers, and she wasn't sure she could still feel her feet.

His lips were full and soft, and his tongue tasted of coffee as it swept inside her mouth.

Oh, the man could kiss. Her toes were practically curling in her sneakers as his wide hands drew her up and held her against him even as she melted. Instinctively she reached out and grabbed his shoulders, holding on, fingers gripping his shirt. He shifted, letting her down a little, his hand dropping to the hollow of her back, and she did what she'd wanted to do for days. She slipped her hands into the thick mass of his hair, luxuriating in the soft fullness, the untamed wildness of it.

He groaned. She shifted her weight and…

Her foot went through a board.

She cried out, losing her balance. Branson tore his mouth from hers and pulled her firmly into his arms, his face full of alarm. "Not as sturdy as we thought," he said, backing up a few steps away from the weak spot. Jessica hadn't even had time to be afraid. One moment she'd been kissing him; the next she'd been yanked against his body while his face paled.

She looked over the railing. It was a long, long way down. Dizzying, even. If both her feet had gone through…she would have fallen straight down to the rocky ground below.

"Let's get back inside," he said firmly, leading her back the way they'd come, opening the door and practically shoving her inside. Once he'd secured the door again, he let out a breath. "Okay. That was unexpected."

She didn't know if he meant the near accident or the kiss, and she wasn't about to ask him. Both events had her feeling off balance and speechless.

"I'm fine, really," she assured him, startled by his still-pale face while her heart pounded from the adrenaline. "It was just one foot."

"We shouldn't have gone out there at all. Shouldn't have..." His stormy eyes caught hers. "I shouldn't have kissed you. I'm sorry. I don't know what came over me."

Her feelings were momentarily hurt. He was apologizing for kissing her, as if she hadn't been there, just as involved as he. He wasn't solely responsible. She lifted her chin. "Are you sorry because you regret it or sorry because my foot went through the wood? Just asking if I should take this personally or not."

His lips fell open as he stared. "Take this personally? Jess, you could have fallen. A fall like that would have killed you."

His face was so tortured right now that her heart squeezed. Considering his past, of course this was upsetting. But she stepped a bit closer, enough that she could put her hand on his forearm. "What I'm asking is if this is about the danger or if you think kissing me was a mistake."

He didn't answer. She watched as he swallowed, his throat bobbing with the effort as she slid her hand to his wrist and twined her fingers with his.

"Kissing me isn't wrong, Bran," she said softly. "It's just a kiss. I liked it."

His thumb rubbed over hers. She was sure he didn't realize he was doing it, but it did strange things to her insides. "You shouldn't say things like that."

"Why? We're adults. Kissing is…kissing." She tried a flirty smile, unsure of how it really looked, figuring she probably appeared awkward. But she was trying. She wanted to keep this light. And she wanted to kiss him again. There was nothing wrong with that, was there?

So she eased herself even closer and lifted her other hand to his face. His eyes closed as her thumb rubbed over the crest of his cheekbone, a soft caress to a man who appeared to need it desperately. She wondered how long it had been since he'd been touched. If there'd been anyone since his wife's death…considering how he hid himself away, she somehow doubted it. Was what just happened the first physical intimacy he'd had in two years?

"Branson," she whispered, and his eyes opened. "Please kiss me again. Please."

There was a pause where she didn't think he was going to, and then he dipped his head and touched his lips to hers.

It was different from the kiss outside, which had been windswept and turbulent and unexpected. This was gentle, deliberate, decimating. Jess leaned into him as he folded her into an embrace, and kissed her with a thoroughness that left her breathless and wanting more.

But more was too much, at least for today. So she contented herself with the kiss, the nuances of it, the way he delved deeply and then retreated to nibble at the corner of her mouth, stealing her breath. The way his broad hand curled around the tender skin of her neck, where her pulse drummed heavily. How his body was solid and warm and unrelenting in all the right places, while his lips were soft and persuasive.

She was the one to break away finally, a bit overwhelmed by her own feelings and desires. If it were up to her, they'd christen the lighthouse right here and now, or perhaps dash over the rocky knoll to the house and find their way to his bed. Those desires were natural and exciting, but it was different with Bran. He wasn't the type to sleep with a woman impulsively, or to simply slake a thirst. Not after what he'd been through. So she stepped away, bit down on her lower lip, hoping to memorize his taste, and took a deep, yet shaky, breath.

"You're some kisser," she said, trying a smile. "Please don't apologize for that."

He turned away and faced the windows, looking out over the ocean, and cleared his throat. She smiled a little to herself as she recognized the moment for what it was. She wasn't the only one aroused from that kiss. Secretly, she was glad that stopping was difficult for him, too.

"You're not so bad yourself," he replied, his voice rough. "But—"

"Don't say but," she interrupted. "Let's just leave it as a very nice moment between two very nice people, with no regrets or expectations."

He turned his head to look at her. "Is that possible?"

"I think so. Besides, you're not ready. I'm not stupid, Bran."

He nodded. "We should go back down. The afternoon's getting on."

He opened the trapdoor, and Jess started down the stairs. They were plunged into darkness again as he shut the door, blocking out the light. The small window partway up gave them a sliver of grayness to navigate by, and then they reached the bottom. Branson opened the door and Jess stepped outside into the blustery wind, while he followed and locked the door behind him.

She shouldered her bag and gathered up her gear. Without asking or offering, Bran carried her folding chair and one of her bags to her car, which sat at the end of the lane—she still didn't park at the house. Didn't feel it would be right.

They were nearly to her car when she let out a breath and said what had been on her mind for the last ten minutes. "Bran?"

"Yeah?"

"You weren't thinking of…her, were you? Your wife? When we were kissing?"

And then she held her breath. She could understand him not being ready. Could understand if she was the first sexual contact he'd had since losing Jennie. But she did not want to be a stand-in. Bran didn't have much of a poker face. She peered up at him, hoping she could tell if he were lying.

He didn't look at her, but faced straight ahead. "No," he said firmly. "No, I was not thinking of her when I kissed you."

She should have been relieved. But the underlying anger in his voice killed whatever joy she might have felt.

Because maybe he hadn't been thinking of his dead wife. But he wasn't happy about it, either. And that left her exactly nowhere.

CHAPTER FIVE

BRAN DIDN'T GO to the lighthouse anymore. He had no problem with Jessica setting up there, and he sometimes caught glimpses of her, but he didn't watch from the balcony or take her food or ask if she'd like to go inside.

He'd kissed her, for God's sake.

He poured himself another coffee and wandered through the kitchen, aimless. He'd wanted to be a hermit, to go somewhere isolated and alone to work things out in his head. And it had been fine for a few months. He'd popped into Jeremy's on occasion, and Tori made sure he wasn't too solitary. He hadn't come to any conclusions, but at least he'd been able to stop pretending that he was okay. He didn't have to go through the motions for anyone. And if he wanted to fall apart, he was free to do so without being watched by friends, colleagues and even the press.

Now he was getting a bit of cabin fever.

Maybe it was the June weather. The days were warmer and things were really starting to grow. Tulips and daffodils had come and gone in his perennial beds, and the hostas were showing their broad, striped leaves. Now other perennials he couldn't name were sprouting in his flower beds, along with weeds. There was some kind of leafy plant growing in a clump behind the house that he had no idea what to do with.

He could garden, he supposed. Just because he never had didn't mean he couldn't.

But not today. Today was bleak and rainy, a gloomy cover of cloud hanging over the coast while rain soaked into his green lawn. He looked at the lighthouse and wished the light was there, flashing into the distance. Instead, it just looked cold and neglected.

There was the section of platform where Jessica's foot had gone through, scaring him to death.

The railing that wasn't safe, either. How easily she could have lost her balance and gone through it. His heart seized just thinking about the possibility.

The hand holding his coffee paused halfway to his lips as a scene flashed into his head.

A scene. With characters, and danger and a question only his writer's brain could answer. *Did she fall or was she pushed?*

Excitement zipped through his veins. He took his coffee and headed straight for the den and his laptop. This time when he booted up, he didn't bother opening email or his browser. He went right to his word processing program and started typing.

When he looked up later, two hours had passed, his coffee was cold, his brain was mush and he was equal parts relieved and scared.

He could still write.

He could maybe move on.

And he was still carrying guilt with him. Only this time he didn't want to feel guilty for doing something that used to be as natural to him as breathing.

After saving the document, he heated his coffee in the microwave, looked at the time and grabbed a muffin from a plastic container on the kitchen counter. He'd missed lunch but he didn't care. He'd written. Maybe not a lot, but it was a start. And he was standing in his kitchen with two-hour-old coffee, a just-okay blueberry muffin and no one to share his excitement with.

He could call Jeremy, but Jeremy worried too much and would tell Tori, who would ask too many questions in her quest to be helpful. Besides, he wasn't sure either of them would truly get it. He thought about Cole, who totally understood loss and moving on, but who was a workaholic who scheduled his recreation time like part of his to-do list. Bran wasn't close with his own family, and the last people he wanted to talk to about making this kind of a step were his in-laws. They loved him. He loved them. But their relationship was so painful now, tinged with grief and regret. They hadn't spoken since he'd moved into the house.

He picked up his phone and sent a text instead. It said simply:

I wrote today!

There was no immediate answer, so he finished his muffin, pondering more about the kernels of the story he'd begun. Right now he had only a scene. He wasn't even sure who the villain was, or the story question. There was no outline, no solid plot. But there was something. There was a victim and a suspicious death, and that was definitely something to a mystery writer.

His phone vibrated on the countertop, making a loud noise in the silence. He picked it up and saw it was Jess, replying to his text.

That's wonderful! Happy for you!

And she truly was. He knew because she understood.

His thumbs paused as he tried to come up with a suitable response.

It is because of you. I have a dead body at the bottom of the lighthouse. Not sure if she was pushed or if she fell. All because you scared the heck out of me last week.

The phone vibrated in his hand.

I'm trying not to be alarmed by any of that. Seriously, congrats on catching a glimpse of your muse. Give her time to come back to you slowly. Accept what she offers you. Soon you will be good friends again.

His heart warmed. She had such a way of putting things, of seeing the good side, of offering hope. And that was something he hadn't expected to have for a very long time.

Still, she was right about one thing the other day. Writing a scene was one thing. Moving forward on a personal level was something he was not ready for. Her question had rocked him to the soles of his feet. No, he hadn't been thinking of Jennie when he'd kissed Jess. And that had hurt him deeply. He didn't ever want to forget the woman he'd loved. The mother of his child.

He didn't want to fall in love again, either. If he'd learned anything, it was that life was precious and nothing was guaranteed. He'd loved Jennie, loved their son with all his heart. He'd promised to do better for them than his father had done for him. And then he'd done the exact same thing: he'd put work ahead of his family. And the consequences were devastating. He never wanted to go through that again.

Which brought his thoughts around full circle to Jess.

He liked her. A lot. And there was no denying he was attracted to her. That kiss the other day had awakened something in him that had been dormant for too long. It was a good thing that she was just here for the summer. Someone passing through his life, not sticking around. There was a little bit of safety in that, after all. The confusing thing was how to proceed. Should they be friends? Could they be friends without being physical? Could they be physical without falling in love? Because the last thing he wanted to do was set up unreasonable expectations.

Bran figured he was probably overthinking, so he pushed the thoughts aside and went out to the lighthouse instead. He walked around the perimeter, examined the ground around the base, looked up at the platform high above. Brow furrowed, he took the key and went inside, then lugged the single mattress up the stairs, trying to ignore the dust and probably mold that had settled into it. Once outside, he gingerly felt his way to the railing, making sure not to get too close. And then he tipped the damp and heavy mattress over the edge, seeing where it fell.

A person would be heavier, but the placement at the bottom was what he was after.

He went inside, shut the trapdoor and timed how long it took him to get back outside and to where the "body" lay. Satisfied, he dragged the mattress back inside and left it on the floor in a puff of dust.

It really was a shame that it was in such disrepair. Had the previous owners not cared? The house was three thousand square feet of elegance and had been lovingly cared for. The lighthouse, full of history, was a derelict.

Maybe he could be the one to restore it.

Energized, he trotted back to the house. First, he wanted more words. There were some adjustments that needed to be made in the scenes he'd just written. And after that, he'd start researching restoration.

He didn't need to think about Jessica Blundon

at all. He just needed something to keep him occupied, and this was perfect.

Jess spent one more week sketching at the lighthouse, but Bran never came out anymore. She didn't even see him on his balcony, or in his gardens. It was as if he was deliberately avoiding her ever since they'd shared that kiss. Or kisses, rather. There'd been two. One impulsive. The other not. He wasn't pleased about either.

Now she had started painting, and while she missed sitting out in the sunshine, she was enjoying her time in her makeshift studio with the familiar smells and tools around her. Her loft in Chicago was bigger, but this suited her just fine. She had only to take a few steps to make a cup of tea or something to eat. The ocean was outside her door. And while she didn't want to overstay her welcome, Jeremy and Tori had become friends and she saw them often. Baby Rose was growing each day, and Tori was starting to look slightly more rested as she got more sleep. Jeremy doted on her in a way that was so sweet it made Jess's heart hurt.

She'd never had a love like that. She'd loved, sure. But each time that particular blossom had bloomed, it had ended up wilting, too, until there was nothing left but to move on. She tried not to overthink it. Ana had always said that there was no one good enough. That no one understood what it meant to be a creative. Or they were jealous of her talent. Compliments all, but lonely just the same. And each time a relationship ended, a little bit of hope for a family of her own died, too.

But she could live a fulfilled life just the same. It was all about being happy with what you had, rather than spending too much time wishing. Wishing just led to disappointment.

Right now she was working on her first painting, starting small, working from the sketch she'd made of the door and the daisies beside it. She wanted to do a whole series here, not just of the lighthouse but of the whole experience of being on the South Shore.

But she missed Bran. She'd be lying to herself to deny it.

A week passed. The end of June approached and she worked long hours, taking time only for walks and meals. She spoke to her agent and negotiated with Tori to stay at the boathouse until the end of August. Then she, her sketches and paintings would head back to Chicago. She could finish there in her own studio.

Finally, on a Friday night, Tori asked her up to the house for dinner. Jess pressed her phone to her ear and asked the tough question. "Is Branson going to be there?"

"No," Tori replied. "He's gone to Halifax for something. It's just us. And I'm not even cooking. Jeremy is stopping for fish and chips on the way home."

Her stomach growled. That sounded so good... "Okay, then. Let me clean up and I'll be there. What should I bring?"

Tori laughed. "Yourself?"

"How about wine? Or can you have any?"

"I can sneak a glass. I've got enough milk expressed to feed Rose. That would be lovely."

So Jessica washed up, changed into a simple floral maxi dress, twisted her hair into a messy topknot and grabbed not only a bottle of pinot grigio but a basket of early-season strawberries. They'd make a simple dessert after their takeout meal.

When she arrived at the house, Tori was outside in the backyard, putting plates on the patio table while Rose kicked and played in a playpen covered with a fine mosquito net. "Are the bugs bad?" Jess asked, handing over the wine.

"No. I'm just overly cautious, I think, and hate the thought of an itchy bite on Rose's delicate skin. To be honest, I just love eating dinner outside. Unless it's raining, we eat out here nearly every night."

"You guys are the cutest."

Tori beamed. "Do you think? Wait'll I tell

Jeremy. 'Cutest' isn't something he's used to being called."

They went into the kitchen briefly and Tori put the wine in the fridge to chill, then put the berries on a shelf. "You know, six months ago I was living in a tiny little house and working at the Sandpiper. It's hard to believe this is my life now. I'm so lucky. I'm so *happy*."

They went back outside, sitting in the shade next to Rose's playpen. "How did you and Jeremy meet, then? He's from New York, right?"

"Connecticut originally." She reached inside the netting and handed Rose a ring with keys on it. The baby shook her fist and the keys rattled, making her even more excited. "He came here on business last summer and stayed at the Sandpiper. Two weeks later he was gone." She met Jess's gaze. "When he came back at the end of November, he discovered I was pregnant."

"Oh, wow." Jess sat back in her chair. "So you got married?"

Tori laughed. "If only it were that simple. But we did in the end. After we fell in love with each other. And now here we are. We're going to split time between here and New York. Jeremy's actually looking for a place for us on Long Island. He'll commute in to work. And he has a flat right by Central Park."

Three residences and all of them pricey. "I didn't realize he was so rich."

"Neither did I. He and Bran and Cole are all loaded. I call them the Billionaire Babies."

Jessica coughed. "Did you say Billionaire Babies?"

Tori nodded. "You didn't know?"

"I knew Branson was successful, but a billionaire?"

Rose started to fuss so Tori took her out of the playpen and sat her on her lap. She straightened her little dress as she chatted. "Oh, most of his money is family money. To be honest, I don't think their childhoods were great. Lots of money, not much love and high expectations."

A billionaire. A freaking billionaire. And yet he was living proof that money was no guarantee of happiness. He'd lost the people most important to him. No money could protect him from that. The conversation they'd had during their picnic came back to her. She'd teased him about servants...but she'd only been teasing. He'd been serious. Of course he'd had servants. Hot embarrassment slid into her cheeks.

"Does it change things?" Tori asked.

"What do you mean?"

Tori rubbed Rose's back and a little burp came out, making them laugh. Tori cuddled her close but then leveled her gaze on Jess.

"Knowing he's rich. Does it change how you feel about him?"

Jess frowned. "Why would it? I couldn't care less about his bank balance. Besides, I barely know him."

Tori was quiet for a long moment, and Jess felt her cheeks warm. "Are you sure?" Tori asked.

"Sure about not caring about his money, or sure about barely knowing him?"

"About not knowing him," Tori said. "I believe you about the money. To be honest, I found it a little intimidating at first."

Jess sighed. She did, too. She did just fine on her own, and was successful in her own right. But she wasn't megarich. "It doesn't matter either way. He's still grieving for his wife and son. Even if I were interested, he's not."

"So nothing's happened? Nothing at all?"

Tori sounded so hopeful. And Jess had never been one to kiss and tell, but she hadn't really had a girlfriend since Ana. She missed having someone to confide in, and Tori knew Bran better than most. Would it hurt to get someone else's perspective? Was she overthinking all of this or getting it wrong? Because she certainly hadn't been able to get him off her mind.

"We kissed," she admitted, the heat in her cheeks now a burning flame. "But just one time, really. He hasn't spoken to me since."

Tori leaned forward, her eyes flashing. "Oh, that's wonderful news!"

Jess laughed in spite of herself. "How do you reckon? I mean, we're not speaking." Besides the text about writing again, she thought to herself. But that didn't really count.

"Bran wasn't even leaving the house. Jeremy was so worried. The fact that he kissed you? Major progress." Suddenly her face fell. "Oh, I'm sorry, Jessica. I didn't take into account how you were feeling about it. Are you doing okay?"

She sighed. "Yeah, I'm okay. I mean…it was pretty great. But I could tell he was mad at himself after, you know? So it didn't really end well."

"Well, something happened to him to light a fire beneath his butt. He told Jeremy he was going to Halifax for a few days to look into restoration of the lighthouse. He said it's in rough shape, and he wants to fix it up."

Jess sat up straighter. "Are you kidding?"

"Not at all."

Jess was gutted. The lighthouse was beautiful as it was, strong and scarred. Granted, the platform at the top could use repairs, and it was dirty inside, but restoration? For what purpose? It would be covering up all its character. It would be as if he were erasing anything that smacked of the two of them together. And that stung. Even if it didn't go anywhere, she could take a nice memory away from that afternoon. She certainly didn't feel the need to paint over it.

In fact, the whole encounter had enhanced her approach to the paintings. Imbued her with a new emotion that would only be beneficial.

She was still stewing when Jeremy came through the house to the backyard through the house, carrying a huge paper bag in his hands. "Someone call for dinner?"

The smell of fries and fish filled the air, and Jess's stomach rumbled again. She was hungry, and what Bran did with the lighthouse was his business, wasn't it? She had absolutely no say. She had her sketches. Branson Black could do whatever he liked. And now she knew he had the money to do it. Despite the big house and beautiful car, she'd had no inkling he was so wealthy. He wasn't flashy about it. She'd give him that much.

Jeremy laid out the meal, and Jessica went inside to get the wine and the corkscrew that Tori had put on the island. When she went back outside, Jeremy was holding Rose and Tori was filling her plate with food. It was so perfectly domestic. She wondered if Bran had experienced these moments with his wife and baby.

Surely he had. And she could understand how a person might not come back from a loss like that.

She was sympathetic. But it didn't mean she was willing to be...disposable.

Pasting on a smile, she took a takeout container and emptied it onto her plate. It certainly smelled delicious. Jeremy put Rose in her playpen again and worked on opening the wine. She'd stumbled onto the sticking point that had been nagging at her ever since that day at the lighthouse. He'd treated her as if she was disposable. And maybe he was angry at himself. But there was no question she'd felt cast aside, and that hurt. After going through most of her life feeling invisible, being seen and discarded hurt even more than not being noticed at all. This was why she didn't put herself out there anymore. It just wasn't worth it.

But she wasn't going to let it ruin her evening, so she shook some vinegar on her fish, picked up her fork and dug in. It was perfectly flaky, the tartar sauce creamy and flavorful, and there was a plastic dish of coleslaw for them to share. The conversation turned to other things, namely Jeremy's search for a property for the third in their trio, Cole, who wanted something he could use as a corporate retreat. So far not much had turned up on Jeremy's radar.

When the meal was over, Jess carried the dirty dishes back to the kitchen and returned to the table with the carton of freshly washed berries. As the evening cooled, they talked and Jess had another glass of wine while Tori gave Rose a prepared bottle.

Jess was barely over thirty, but the family scene had her biological clock ticking madly tonight. When Rose was finished eating, she took her from Tori's arms to give her a break and to get baby snuggles. She hadn't thought about wanting children a whole lot, but spending time with Rose these past weeks had made her wonder. She smelled so good; like milk and baby lotion and fresh cotton. The fact that the baby settled so easily into her arms made her feel motherly and strangely competent. It took no time at all before Rose's little lashes were resting on her cheeks and her lips opened slightly, slack in slumber.

She was such a sweet little thing. And for the first time in years, Jessica let herself really yearn for what she didn't have. What she might never have. And she held on tight.

CHAPTER SIX

THE SUN WAS setting and Jeremy had just lit the citronella torches when the slamming of a car door echoed through the still evening air. Jess frowned and looked over her shoulder, but couldn't see anything. A few moments later, Tori met her gaze and nodded. *Bran*, she mouthed, and Jess swallowed tightly. She was still thinking about the kiss, and thinking about him restoring the lighthouse. She bit down on her lip. She couldn't escape the notion that he was fixing it because he wanted to essentially cover up what had happened between them. A fresh coat of paint and some new lumber would erase a lot, wouldn't it?

"Good evening, Bran," Tori said softly. "Come on in and have a seat. You want a drink?"

"Naw, I'm good for now." He came into the circle and nodded at Jess, his gaze settling on her and the baby in her arms. "Jessica. I didn't know you'd be here."

Or else he wouldn't have come. She summoned her pride. "Likewise."

He hesitated, but then sat. "Sorry. I didn't mean that the way it sounded."

Her cheeks heated and she let out a breath. "It's okay. No biggie."

Jeremy jumped into the middle of the awkwardness. "So, Bran. What brings you by? How was the trip to Halifax?"

"Good." Bran smiled, and it transformed his face. Jess realized she'd hardly ever seen him smile, and that when he did she forgot just about everything in her head. His face completely changed, relaxing and opening more, while his soft lips curved beneath his beard.

The beard that had tickled her chin and neck not long ago. She pushed the thought away.

"You're really going to change the lighthouse?" Jess asked, trying hard to keep censure out of her voice. She had no claim to it. Her creative "tingles" held no weight when it came to what he chose to do with the lighthouse It didn't mean she had to be happy about it.

He nodded. "Yeah. It's in pretty rough shape. I honestly think it's been neglected for decades. First we're going to make it safe. Then we'll worry about cosmetics."

"You don't think all the changes will erase its character?"

"If I leave it as it is, it'll rot away. I don't want it to disappear."

"Not to mention how it might work against resale value," Jeremy pointed out, lifting his glass as he sat in a padded chair. "Sometimes selling points become liabilities real fast."

Jess's gaze met Bran's. "You're thinking of selling already?"

When he shook his head, she was relieved, though she couldn't say why. Her life wasn't here, and there was nothing really between them anyway. Why should she care if he stayed or not?

"No," he answered firmly. "I don't plan on selling for a while. Even if I go back to New York eventually, this is a great place to retreat to, you know?"

"What made you decide to take on the lighthouse, anyway?" Tori asked.

"A discovery that the platform and railing at the top aren't safe." He didn't look at her this time, but his smile had vanished. "Half the boards are rotted. The lamp is fine and won't be used again anyway, but I've got someone coming out to have a look at the foundation and make sure that structurally we're sound. It's been neglected. It's a beautiful piece of history that's mostly been abandoned. At least maybe I can be a better steward to it."

She wanted to be angry or at the very least annoyed that he was going to paint over the battle scars the building had sustained over the years. There were stories there. Stories he should appreciate as a writer. But it was hard to argue with wanting to take care of something and cherish it.

"I think I got used to its weathered look," she said quietly.

Now he looked at her, his gaze inscrutable. "I know. But it's about safety. The last thing I want is for someone to get hurt."

She couldn't look away. He said it while looking directly in her eyes. And the moment on the platform spun out in her mind—the wind, the moment her foot went through the rotten board and the instant freezing fear, and the feel of his strong body against hers as he held her tight.

He might be able to walk away from their kisses that day without any problem, but she couldn't.

She was smart enough to realize that she was falling for Branson Black, the most unavailable man she'd ever met.

Dammit.

Rose squirmed a bit in her arms, and she finally broke eye contact. "Shh…" She adjusted the weight of the baby in an effort to keep her settled, but Tori got up and came to retrieve

Rose. "Her naps in the early evening are getting shorter. Which is a blessing for me. Now she'll stay up until about eleven, and sleep through until five. It feels like absolute heaven."

Jess's arms felt cold and empty without the baby, a thought she didn't want to delve too far into. Instead, she smiled and got to her feet. "I really should go anyway. I'm up early these days to work. But thank you once again for dinner. I'm going to have to have you down to the boathouse for a meal soon."

"That would be lovely!" Tori snuggled a fussy Rose against her shoulder.

Of course Jess didn't quite know where she was going to seat everyone, now that the main floor space was transitioned into a studio. But no matter. They'd figure it out. Maybe it would turn into a picnic on the beach.

Bran stood as well. "I'll walk you home," he said.

Jeremy laughed. "Sure, bro. It's like a hundred yards to the boathouse. You're not fooling anyone."

Jess blushed and Bran stared at his friend. "Shut up, Jer," he said mildly. But Jeremy merely chuckled and didn't say anything more. Jess was cluing into the fact that Bran was a still-waters-run-deep kind of guy, and that when he spoke, people generally listened. It was a trait that could be frustrating but that she admired, too.

This time when they reached the boathouse she invited him in. "Why don't you come in for a bit? It's still early."

He stepped inside and took off his shoes, leaving them on the tiny mat by the door.

"You know, I've never been in here," he mused, peeking ahead. "It's tiny but kind of cozy."

"I think it's somewhere between six and seven hundred square feet. Single bedroom, bathroom, living room, small kitchen. But as a getaway, it's sweet." She led him through to the living room and smiled as his eyes widened. Her easel was set up, and a small covered table held brushes, paint, palette knives and an apron that was smattered with a rainbow of colors. To her it was the most comforting sight in the world. To him, it must look like chaos.

"Wine? I have white and red. I might have a beer in here somewhere."

"None for me. I'll take water if you have it."

She looked at him closely. Realized she'd never actually seen him have a drink other than lemonade or coffee, which he seemed to drink constantly. "I have sparkling."

"That'd be great."

She went to the fridge for the bottle and

poured some into a glass with ice, then handed it to him. "Do you mind if I do?" she asked, motioning toward the half-empty bottle of red on the counter.

"Of course not." He smiled at her. "So this is your studio."

"For now. It's a lot smaller than my place in Chicago, but it suits my needs better than I ever expected."

She poured some wine into a glass and turned to him. "I was only going to stay a week or two, you know. Move on like I've been doing for months. And then Tori offered me this place… and it's been wonderful. The peace and quiet. The cute towns and scenery. I understand why you chose it to…" She paused, feeling suddenly awkward. "Well, to regroup, I suppose. Or recharge. I know it's working for me."

"Yeah." He hesitated a moment, then said, "Are you upset about me restoring the lighthouse? I know you've used it as inspiration."

Jess took a sip of her wine. "I was at first. For a few reasons that were nothing but selfish. But what you said about being a steward is right. And so is safety. I'm so sorry I scared you that day."

"It wasn't your fault."

She gestured to the front door. "Do you want to sit outside? There's more room."

"Sure."

The little porch gave a glimpse of the water, and as evening settled around them, they sat in the Adirondack chairs and let the soft sound of the waves soak in. He sipped his water; she savored the wine and let out a happy sigh. The sky turned shades of lilac, peach and pink, a natural palette that filled Jess's soul with comfort.

"It's beautiful tonight."

"Yeah. There's something about the ocean that just calms me and energizes me at the same time."

He let out a long sigh. "It soothes. The sea just is. It crashes and rolls, it waves and breaks and chases the sand. Twice a day it moves in, then retreats, leaving treasures behind. When our world is small and filled with worries, the ocean is endless and constant."

She shouldn't have been surprised at his being poetic; he was a writer after all. But the description touched her just the same. "Is your world small and filled with worries, Bran?" She'd held her breath as he spoke, but now let it out slowly.

"Not as much as it used to be. The sea has worked its magic on me, too."

"I'm glad."

"And so have you."

Her breath stopped. "Me?"

He looked over at her, his eyes black in the growing twilight. "Yes, you. I'm sorry for the way I acted that day." She didn't need to ask which day he meant. "I was feeling guilty, and mad at myself, and I took it out on you. You did nothing wrong, Jess."

She held his gaze. "Neither did you, Bran. You just weren't ready for it. But it wasn't wrong." She reached for his hand. "I might be overstepping here, so please don't be angry when I say very bluntly that you are not married to her anymore."

His throat bobbed as he swallowed, then he squeezed her fingers. "I know. But I'm in that spot where I feel as if moving on means I'm forgetting her."

"You'll never forget her. Allowing yourself to have a life and move on doesn't mean forgetting."

"In my head I know that. But that day, I reacted. I reacted when I kissed you and I reacted when I put you in your car to leave. It was wrong and I owe you an apology."

"Accepted. And I'm thrilled you're writing again."

She thought he would pull his hand away, but he kept his fingers twined with hers and she tried not to think too much about it.

"Me, too. It's slow going, but it's a start. I haven't said anything to anyone else, though. I don't want to set up expectations."

"Not even your agent?"

"Not yet. I want to have a solid start before I talk to him about it. It's early days. But one of the reasons I went to Halifax was to visit the archives and do a little digging."

"And did you find out anything interesting?"

"Lots. Like rumors of U-boats off the coast in the forties. The presence of spies during the war. It's feeding my muse, and she's been hungry a long time."

"Looks like this place is kind of key for both of us. Two lost souls, huh?"

"I'm not feeling so lost right now."

His dark gaze had her insides fluttering again, so she got up and held out her hand. "Can I get you a refill?"

Slowly, ever so slowly, he pushed himself up from the chair. He was so tall, and in the dark, with his beard and hair, he looked intimidating and dangerous. But not truly dangerous... more enigmatic and sexy.

"I can get it."

He took the glass and went inside while Jessica let out a long, slow breath. She was not immune to him in any way. She'd been prepared to be angry with him about the restoration. To let it be the thing that kept him at arm's length. Instead, he'd stated his reasons and the distance evaporated. Every time she set up some sort of block, he knocked it down with ease.

She was here only for the summer. He was not for her. And she seemed to lack the will-power to push him away.

He returned with a full glass and instead of sitting, went to the railing and looked out over the sloping lawn and shrubs to the beach below. "You wanna walk?" he asked.

A moonlight walk on the beach? Could she possibly say no?

"That would be lovely," she whispered.

He drank his water and put the glass down on the arm of the wooden chair, and then held out his hand. She took it, hoping he couldn't tell that hers was shaking. What a ninny she was, trembling over holding hands at her age. It wasn't like she hadn't ever been in love and he was some sort of first. He was just…different.

Like now, with his hair blowing back from his face in the ocean breeze. He'd left his sandals inside her door and his feet were bare as they approached the silky white sand. She tugged on his hand to stop him for a moment while she slipped off her Vans and let her toes sink in, the sand still warm from the day's sun.

He still had her hand. She swallowed tightly

and kept her fingers tangled with his. Admitting that she'd been lonely was hard. She considered herself strong and self-reliant. She always had been, with a good dose of obstinacy thrown in for good measure. But she'd needed this, she realized. Even more so since she lost her best friend. She needed contact and intimacy. Clearly Branson Black was not Mr. Right. But he was doing a pretty good job being Mr. Right Now.

"I never imagined soft white sand like this up here," she said, her steps lazy and squishy in the thick sand. "I always imagined it farther south. In the clear waters of the Caribbean. But this is amazing."

He was quiet for a few moments, then lifted his chin and drew in a deep breath of sea air. "I met Jennie in Nova Scotia. Not here. On the other side of the province. I decided to take a road trip and drove north through Maine, took the ferry from New Brunswick to Digby, and ended up on the Fundy coast. She was working the summer doing marine research. My plans to travel to Prince Edward Island and Cape Breton just disappeared. Once I met her, that was it."

"She was from here?"

"No, she was on some university grant summer research program with Boston University. I was still living in Connecticut. For nine months we drove back and forth and saw each other on weekends. And once she graduated I asked her to marry me."

"You were young."

He nodded. Breakers swept over the sand, brushing their feet, and Jess mulled over the fact that he was telling her about his wife while they were holding hands. Still, she wasn't going to interrupt. She was curious, and she got the feeling this was not something he talked about often.

"We were, though she was younger than me. We ended up with a two-year engagement and pulled out all the stops for the wedding." He looked over at her. "I would have been happy with the courthouse, but if you knew Jennie…" His smile was sad. "I wanted to give her everything she desired. And I could, so I did."

"She was lucky to have you, Bran." Jess squeezed his hand as they kept taking lazy steps up the beach.

"Was she? Because I got caught up in myself and didn't cherish her enough. I have regrets, Jessica. More than you know."

She stopped and pulled on his hand, making him stop too as she looked up into his face. "I think whenever someone dies, we all have regrets of some sort. You loved her. Maybe you weren't perfect, but you loved her. That's so clear to see in the way you talk about her."

"I did." He sighed. "Jennie was my home. The warm, loving space I didn't have as a child. And I blew it. I was angry about the accident for a long time, and then the sadness threatened to pull me under. Now I'm wanting to start living again, and it feels so strange to be doing it without her. Without our baby, too. God, he was the sweetest thing." His voice thickened and he cleared his throat. "I hope you never have to go through anything like that in your life. I wouldn't wish it on my worst enemy."

He turned and they started walking again, while Jess's thoughts were in turmoil. She'd had her share of loss; not just Ana but of her adopted mother, too. Her dad was still around but had remarried, and they weren't that close. And while her life growing up had been okay, she'd always wondered about her birth parents. She knew nothing about them.

"I was adopted when I was two. I don't have memories of before, but I know that CPS stepped in and removed me from my home when I was a year old. After my parents divorced I stayed with my mom. And then she died several years ago. I was nearly engaged once, but he didn't want to wait for me. So I guess we all have something. You're holding on to regrets. I think I'm just used to the people I love not sticking around."

"Damn. I'm sorry. I mean, I'm not particularly close with my family. My dad is a workaholic and a bit… I don't know, cold. And my mom is okay, but we've never been a tight family. Still, I know they're there."

"And they sent you off to boarding school."

"Yeah, but you know what? I met my best friends in the world. It ended up being the best thing that could have happened. Cole and Jeremy became my family."

She smiled a little. "You certainly seem to have good memories."

"The best." He sighed. "You know, my life's been a bit charmed. Yeah, I lost Jennie and Owen, but we loved each other. I'm blessed to have had that, I guess."

They'd stopped again, and she turned to face him and put her arms around his middle, wrapping him in a hug. What a bittersweet blessing, to have found perfection and to lose it so young.

"Hey," he said softly, and his wide, warm hand came to rest on the middle of her back.

She sniffled. "Sorry. I just thought you needed a hug. Or that I needed to give you one."

"It's okay. You can hug me."

And his other arm came around her and hugged her back.

* * *

Bran drank in the scent of her hair, something soft and floral that mixed with the salty tang of the sea. She was so warm, and so very, very generous. What she'd said about her childhood was surprising. He'd imagined her having this warm and picture-perfect family, completely well-adjusted and loving. But she'd had her share of heartbreak, too, and yet she still found a way to be...open.

It took a certain strength to be able to do that. And something special to make him respond to it, after months of numbness.

Jennie would have liked her. It should feel odd to have such a thought, but somehow it wasn't. Jennie had had that sweetness wrapped in strength, too.

It felt so good to be held.

He pulled her closer against him, let his hand glide over her back, touching warm skin. God, so good, the touch of another human being. She responded, slipping her hands beneath the hem of his T-shirt, and he could feel the gentle marking of her fingernails on his back. He groaned with pleasure, moving his hand down her ribs, his thumb grazing the tender skin between breast and waist through the soft material.

"Bran," she whispered, and his body came alive.

He lowered his head and nuzzled at her ear, pleased when goose bumps erupted on her skin. She tilted her head, and he touched his lips to the soft skin of her neck, up to her jawline, over to her lips, which were slack and waiting for him. The kiss was a wild and wonderful thing, full of passion and acknowledgment of their attraction. She stood up on tiptoe and wrapped her arms around his neck; he lifted her up off her toes and held her flush against his body as he plundered her mouth. Her hands sank into his hair and his pulse leaped. If he wasn't careful, he was going to lay her down on the sand right here and now. At Jeremy's house. He understood now why his lighthouse was the perfect spot for a tryst. A little ocean, some moonlight, add a lot of desire and things had a way of happening.

Her chest heaved with her breathing, and he placed his hand over her heart. He was shocked to discover she wasn't wearing a bra as her small, firm breast pressed against his hand.

His control was on shaky ground.

So he lifted her up in his arms, cradling her close, and started walking toward the water.

He was nearly to his knees when Jessica figured out what he was doing. She pushed against him and started to laugh and protest at the same time. "Bran! No! You are not going to throw me in the water!"

He grinned. "Throw? No. But we need to cool off, and there's only one way I can think of to do that."

She struggling against him some more, but suddenly she was laughing too, and the sound filled his heart with something that felt…joyful. Water splashed up over his knees as the waves rolled in. It was cold; there was definitely going to be some temperature shock. But nature's equivalent of a cold shower was in both their best interests right now.

"Bran!" she exclaimed, as a wave rose up and touched her bottom, making her arch against him.

He laughed, the sound rumbling in his chest before erupting into the evening air. His shorts were wet now, and another step had them in up to his waist. "Ready?" he asked.

"No!" She squealed and twisted in his arms, laughing the whole time. "You are not going to drop me into the ocean. You are not—"

He took one more step, then let her go with a splash. And then he dove under, hoping to cool his jets.

When he surfaced about ten feet away, Jessica had come up and was still spluttering and wiping her hair away from her face. She looked so indignant that he burst out laughing. The look she turned on him was positively venomous, and then she started toward him. When she was five, maybe six feet away, she started splashing him, the water hitting him in the face and he had to stop laughing to keep from getting a mouthful. Instead he turned, stepped toward her and yanked her close, where she couldn't splash anymore.

"You. Are. Incorrigible." She was still laughing but said the last word on a sigh. He kept his arm around her and she kicked up from the bottom, pointing her toes up through the surface. "I can't believe you did that."

"Me either." He let her go, and they bobbed around in the water for a few minutes. His cargo shorts were heavy and his T-shirt uncomfortable, and his legs were already starting to go numb from the cold. Still, he found it hard to be sorry. It had been so long since he'd done anything impulsive or…or fun. Kissing Jessica and then taking a plunge in the Atlantic had been both.

Her dress billowed around her, moving with the waves as she ran her fingers through her hair, which was far darker now that it was wet. It made her skin glow in the moonlight, and her eyes shone at him. Quick as anything, she ducked under the water, the tips of her toes giving a little splash like a mermaid. When she surfaced, she was several feet away, standing hip deep in the water.

The fabric of her dress clung to her skin, highlighting every curve and point, and his mouth went dry. Perhaps a dunking in the sea hadn't been the best plan after all.

Sex would be a mistake. For both of them. Wouldn't it?

To distract himself, he swam out until he started to get tired, and then turned to come back. Jess was treading water a few hundred yards away, as if waiting for him. He swam in, and then they went to shore together. The exertion had helped expend some of his restless energy, and when they got to the shore, they hurried out of the water and onto the beach.

"Come up to the boathouse and towel off. You must be freezing."

No more than she was.

The slow, meandering walk of earlier was replaced by quick steps in the sand, and a shorter angle to the path leading away from the beach. Jessica stopped and grabbed her shoes, and when she stood he noticed her lips were blue from cold. He was shivering, too. The days had been summerlike, but the nights were still chilly and being soaking wet made it even worse. In the space of a few minutes,

they were at the boathouse. He stood on the mat
while she disappeared into the bathroom and
returned with two big, fluffy towels.

She scrubbed her hair and rubbed it over her
arms and legs. He did the same. And wished
her dress wasn't quite so see-through. It wasn't
helping his resolve to keep things nonsexual.

"You're freezing," she said, looking up at
him. "Let me put your things in the dryer."

"I don't exactly have anything to change
into."

Suggestion swirled around them, but Jessica
was the one to break the moment. "I have a
blanket. I know it's not optimal, but you can't
go home like that. Unless you want to go to Jeremy's and ask for a change of clothes."

He lifted an eyebrow. "No, thanks. He'll ask
too many questions."

"Well, then. Hang on."

She disappeared into the bathroom and came
out again with another towel and a soft blanket. She handed him the towel first. "You can
put this on like a skirt, to cover your…sensitive
bits." Her cheeks flushed. "And then wrap the
blanket around you."

He grabbed at the hem of his T-shirt and
swept it over his head, though it stuck to his
shoulders as he pulled it off. He dropped it
on the floor with the first towel, and when he

saw her owlish expression at his bare chest he paused with his fingers on the button of his shorts.

Her cheeks were ruddy now and she turned away. "I'll just go change and then put my stuff in with yours."

A laugh built in his chest as he took off his shorts and secured the towel away from his... what had she called them? Sensitive bits. The blanket was large enough that he wrapped it around himself like a cape. When she emerged from the bedroom, she gathered up his wet clothes and scuttled off to the laundry room. He heard a few beeps and then the low hum of the dryer.

When she came back out, she stopped in the kitchen and put water in her kettle. She'd changed into yoga pants and a soft sweatshirt with paint stains on it. Her hair was starting to dry a little, with bits of natural curl framing her face. He felt like an idiot standing there in a towel and blanket, but what the hell. Nothing about their relationship so far had been ordinary or exactly comfortable.

She looked over at him and laughed. "You look silly."

"I feel silly."

"How about that drink now? I have some Scotch. It might warm you up."

He met her gaze. "I don't drink anymore."

Her face changed. First there was surprise, followed swiftly by embarrassment. Then a growing realization and acceptance. She'd been at his house. To Jeremy's for drinks, but he'd never partaken in anything alcoholic. He didn't make a big deal of it, but he could see her putting the pieces together.

In her blunt fashion, she met his gaze and asked, "Are you an alcoholic?"

CHAPTER SEVEN

BRAN SHRUGGED AS he considered her question. "I don't know. I mean, I don't know if there's an actual criteria I would meet or anything. What I do know is that I was self-medicating to deal with my grief, and I stopped." He hesitated, then decided to be completely honest. "Jennie would be pretty angry with me if she knew I'd turned to alcohol as a coping mechanism."

"What took its place?"

"Getting out of New York. Long walks on the beach. And there were times it was really hard. But I don't keep any in my house, and it makes it easier."

Her lips dropped open and an expression of dismay darkened her face. "Oh, Bran. I gave you a bottle of wine that first day for stress. I'm so sorry."

He waved it away, and nearly dropped the blanket. "Don't be. You didn't know. I've still got it. You're welcome to it sometime when you're visiting."

Her blue eyes touched his. "Will I be visiting?"

It was hard to draw breath. This was the moment where they were maybe becoming a thing. Maybe not sex. Maybe not ever sex. But agreeing to spend time together rather than finding ways not to or chalking it up to coincidence. He nodded slightly. "If you want to."

Her voice was soft. "I'd like that."

He was in danger of moving closer to her again, what with her soft voice and big eyes. "Can we sit down somewhere? I'm feeling kind of ridiculous here."

"Of course!" Her eyes sparkled as she looked at him. "If you can make it around the drop cloth, there's a decent sofa."

He took a look at her current painting as he went by. It was the lighthouse, a full rendering of it, with the soft colors of a sunrise taking shape behind. She was so talented. Even partially completed, the painting seemed to breathe, have a life of its own. "This is beautiful, Jess."

She turned and smiled, then gestured toward the sofa. "Thank you. I'm playing with some colors with that one, and so far I'm liking it."

They sat on the sofa, the plush cushions soft

and comfortable. Jess tucked her feet up underneath herself, relaxed in the corner of the sofa. It was a bit more difficult for him to find a comfortable spot, what with the towel and the blanket. When he finally got situated, she was grinning broadly.

"Don't make fun of me," he said, but his voice held a trace of humor.

"Hey, you were the one who decided to go for the swim, not me."

A sigh escaped his lips. "Only because we were getting too close to..."

His words trailed off. To what? Making a mistake? Making love? Both phrases made his chest tighten. He opted for humor. "To getting naked on Jeremy's beach."

She coughed and laughed at the same time. "Oh, can you imagine if they'd seen..."

He met her gaze evenly. "That dip was my equivalent of a cold shower. I like you, Jess. We have chemistry." She made a sound that was the equivalent of "yeah, we sure do." He held the blanket tightly in his fingers. "I'm not sure sex is in our best interests right now."

She nodded. He wished he didn't notice how full her lips were when they were open just that little bit. Or how her eyes glowed, the little tiny striations of gold and green in the blue making him think of the water at the edge of the lake at Merrick. Or even how her chest rose and fell anytime things heated up between them. Even now, just talking about it and not touching. He was so attuned to her.

Her throat bobbed as she swallowed. "Because of Jennie."

"Yeah. It wouldn't be fair to you."

"Tell me about her, Bran."

He broke eye contact and looked away. Across the room was a matching love seat and one of the pillows was out of place.

But she edged over closer to him and put her hand on his blanket-covered knee. "You need to talk about her. There's no judgment here, Bran. Just talk. Tell me what she was like. Tell me why it's so hard." She squeezed his knee. "I can put on some coffee if you want."

He debated. It was strange thinking about telling the woman you'd almost had sex with about your dead wife. And yet not so strange thinking about telling Jess. Besides, if she knew everything, maybe this horrible, wonderful attraction between them would be nonexistent, and he wouldn't have to worry about making a mistake.

"I don't need coffee," he murmured, resting his hands on his knees. The hem of the towel cut into his pelvis, but he didn't care.

He'd already told her about how he and Jennie had met. But the last year of their marriage...everything had changed.

"The year or so before they died was really different for us," he began. "Owen had been born, and Jennie was such an amazing mother. Like Tori, you know? Loving and caring and tired and fun. She'd spend hours counting his toes and making him laugh. Or just sitting in a rocking chair with him while he slept, wanting to hold on to those first baby days forever." Emotion rose in a wave and he fought it back, not wanting his voice to crack as they spoke.

"Does seeing Tori make it worse for you?" she asked softly.

"Sometimes. It just hurts, seeing Rose grow and knowing that one day soon she'll start having the milestones that Owen never had. But it's not their fault, and he's my best friend. I can't stay away, you know? That's not fair."

She nodded and put her hand on his back, rubbing reassuringly, just like she'd done that day of their picnic on the rock. "But it still hurts."

"Yeah." He took a deep breath. "My career had really taken off by then. My eighth book had just released, and it was a big deal. It hit the lists in its first week, and there was a bunch of appearances set up." He frowned. "I let it go to my head a little bit. I had to be here, there.

Signing books. Doing interviews. I'd gone to our apartment in the city for a few weeks to tackle it all, planning to go home on the weekend in between. But another opportunity came up and I was so tired that I stayed in the city." He tried not to think about the argument he'd had with Jennie about not going home that weekend. She'd been 100 percent right about how he was losing sight of his family.

"The next week Jennie decided to surprise me by driving up from Connecticut. We'd fought about me not being home, and we didn't fight often so it felt so very wrong and off. I had no idea what she was planning until I got the call from the police." His chest cramped so much it nearly made him lose his breath. "I was listed as next of kin, our address the one in New Haven. By the time they reached me, the accident had been cleared and their bodies at the hospital."

His voice finally broke. "I can still see them there, Jess. She was cut up bad. But Owen…he looked like he'd just gone off to sleep. God, I pray he was sleeping and never felt anything. I hope it was all so fast that neither of them suffered or knew what was happening." The well of emotion threatened to strangle him. "They shouldn't have been on the road that night. And they wouldn't have been, if I'd been less full of myself and had gone home as we planned. All she wanted was for us to spend time together as a family, and I was too damned important and busy."

Jess's hand was still rubbing his back. "You blame yourself."

"Of course I do!" he snapped, then let out a breath. "She was my wife. He was my son. The two most important people in the world to me, and I let them down so badly. It should have been me."

"You don't feel you deserve to live."

"No! Yes. I don't know." He shifted away from her hand. "That's the thing, Jess. For a long time, I didn't want to live. And now I do, and I'm left wondering if that makes me a horrible person."

Jess was quiet for a long moment. She finally let out a long breath and angled her body toward him. "When Ana got sick, I was so damned angry. But I didn't cause her cancer. You didn't cause that accident. It was an accident, and they happen."

"But she wouldn't have been on the road at all if I had just gone home like she'd asked."

"And maybe you would have had an accident going home. Would you want Jennie to feel like if she just hadn't asked you to come home that you'd still be alive?"

"Of course not."

"She made a choice, Bran. She could have waited until the weekend. She could have taken a different route, left at a different time. Ana might not have had cancer. What I'm saying is...to think any of this is actually within our control is so flawed. But we look for explanations and blame so we have somewhere to put our grief."

She sniffled and Bran realized she was crying. He wasn't, not this time, but she was, and seeing the wetness on her cheeks and the redness of her eyes nearly undid him. She was so beautiful, inside and out. And he was so very unworthy.

He pulled her close. "You loved her very much."

"More than anyone ever in my life, I think. Even the guy I thought I was going to marry."

"Were you *in* love with her?"

She lifted her head sharply, looked into his eyes. "Oh...no. Not that way."

He chuckled and his arm tightened around her. "Are you surprised I asked?"

"A little. Would it matter to you?"

He shook his head and lifted his shoulders in a shrug. "Why would it? It takes all kinds of love to make the world go round. I never assume anything."

She pushed away and turned on the sofa, sitting with her legs crossed, but she still held his hand. "You know, I didn't expect you to surprise me more than you already have tonight, but you just did." A sweet smile touched her lips. "And every time you surprise me, I like you a little bit more."

She shouldn't like him. It made things harder. And yet he found himself rubbing his thumb over her wrist in a comforting gesture. He could still see the trails tears had made on her cheeks. "I'm sorry you lost her," he said quietly. "She sounds like a wonderful woman."

"She was. And I'm sorry you lost Jennie and Owen. But we're alive, Bran. You and me. Alive and we have lives to live. You can't punish yourself forever. I can't be sad forever."

"Jess…"

"And I feel most alive when I'm with you."

If she kept it up with that soft voice and her big eyes, he was going to have to go for another dip in the sea. He should look away. But he couldn't. Her gaze held him prisoner, his breath shortened as the moment drew out. He was still holding her hand; meanwhile the towel and blanket were feeling rather constrictive.

"I'm not relationship material, Jess. You need to know that. I have nothing to offer someone in that way."

Had she somehow moved closer? "I don't recall asking for a relationship. Or any sort of promises," she whispered. "I don't want them, Bran. I'm here for a matter of weeks, and then I'm going back to my life." She lifted her other hand and cupped his jaw. "Besides, I'm trying this thing where I live in the moment."

In this moment he knew exactly what he wanted. But she asked him first.

"Stay with me," she murmured.

He swallowed around a lump in his throat, his heart pounding with what he was sure were equal measures of arousal and fear.

But he didn't have time to think. Jess shifted and slid one leg over him, so that she was straddling him and he was having serious doubts about the reliability of the towel. She kissed him softly, on the crests of his cheeks, the corners of his eyes, the spot just above his lower lip, until he could hardly breathe. In less than a moment he lifted his arms, sending the blanket cape falling to the side as he wrapped her in a tight embrace. And then they kissed, long, slow, deep, until his brain was swimming with nothing but the feel of her, the scent of her skin, soft and salty from the sea.

When the sofa grew uncomfortable, Jess slid off his lap and held out her hand. He knew what she was asking. Knew it might be a mistake.

But he also knew he had never wanted something so badly. This feeling alive thing was addictive, and he needed another hit. There was one thing standing in his way, though. And it was something he'd never risk.

"Jess, I'm not prepared."

Her cheeks pinkened delightfully, but she shook her head. "It's okay. I've been on the pill for years."

He put his hand in hers and stood, his towel falling away.

Jess tried not to stare, but Bran was standing naked in her living room. Tall and lean, with a small scar on his lower right abdomen, and a soft dusting of hair from his chest down to his navel. She wanted this. But the fierceness with which she wanted him was unfamiliar, and gave her a moment's pause.

Then she met his gaze and he lifted a single eyebrow. She tugged on his hand, leading him past her easel and canvas to the small bedroom and the bottom bunk.

"There's not a lot of head room," she whispered, catching her breath when he came up behind her and his body grazed hers.

"I'm not planning on standing up." His voice was low and seductive, warm at her ear. "Unless you want to."

Oh, my.

Jess took a deep breath and pulled off her hoodie. She still wasn't wearing a bra, and the night air made goose bumps rise on her skin. Wordlessly she shimmied out of her yoga pants, and once she was naked, Bran reached out and pulled her close.

She was afraid. Not of him. But of being overwhelmed.

But he took his time, kissing her, touching her with light strokes, lighting her on fire and making her melt at the same time. His skin was warm on hers, and she marveled at the intimacy of the feeling, skin on skin. When her knees grew weak and he laid her down on the mattress, his eyes found hers in the dim moonlight cast through the window. "Okay?" he asked.

Tears pricked her eyes and she blinked them away. He was so considerate. So gentle. So... everything.

"More than okay," she assured him.

His gaze held hers, his eyes widening for a moment as they came together, key into lock. Jess felt a pang in her heart, the bittersweet knowledge that she'd fallen for a man she couldn't have, or could have but only for a little while.

But living in the moment meant embracing the moment, and she was determined to do that.

So she reached up and looped her hand around his neck, pulling him down for a kiss. If she couldn't have Branson as her love, she could at least have him for her lover. And when their breathing finally slowed and the sweat dried from their skin, she had no regrets.

Jess shifted beneath the blanket, trying not to wake Bran. The sun was barely up, and the light in the bedroom was watery and dim. But it was enough that she could make out his features completely. The bit of hair that was in a tangle on the pillow. His lips, open slightly as he slept, and the way he linked his fingers together over his belly. She liked that the most, as it seemed like a cute little quirk individual to him. He was a back sleeper. She was usually a sprawler, but sprawling was impossible in a bed this size and shared with a man of his build.

They were both naked under the covers. His clothes were still in the dryer, and she was on the inside of the bed, closest to the wall, and hadn't gotten up to pull something on after…

After.

Her chest cramped, in both delicious memory and delightful anticipation. He'd been a thorough, attentive lover. There'd been a moment where something threatened to overwhelm her, and maybe him, too. Their eyes had met and their smiles faded. In that moment sex had become more than just sex. It had become his first time since Jennie. She was sure of that. And for her...

It had been connection. Bone-deep, in-the-blood connection with another human being. For all her live-in-the-moment Zen-ness, deep connections, trust...those were rare occurrences. It was why losing Ana had hurt so badly.

People didn't tend to stay in her life. But this time there was no danger of that. She was going into this with the knowledge and understanding that in a matter of weeks, they'd both be moving on. No surprises, no being blindsided, no one hurt. Bran let out a sigh and something soft and sentimental wound through her at the sound. A smile touched her lips. This summer would be one of healing, for both of them if they were lucky. And they'd be able to look back on this as the summer they made their way back to the living, with fond memories.

Bran stirred and shifted to his side, then his eyes slowly opened. She met his gaze evenly, the smile still on her lips. "Good morning," she whispered.

"Good morning." His cheeks colored a little

and she loved that he was blushing right now, just a hint of pink above his beard.

"You okay?" Mornings-after could be awkward. Things were different in the light of day. Last night they'd been swept up in each other, but now...now they had to navigate the dynamic.

He nodded slightly, then shifted his arm and said, "Come here."

She shifted over and curled in next to his side. His skin was soft and warm, and the smattering of hair on his chest tickled her breasts.

His arm tightened around her. "I'm okay. You?"

She nodded, her cheek rubbing against his shoulder. "Me, too. I was afraid it might be... awkward."

He chuckled, a low sound that moved his chest and made her smile. "It is, a little. I'm very out of practice with mornings-after. But..." He moved his head so that he was looking down at her, and she tilted up her chin. "We've been fairly gentle with each other so far. I figure if we can keep doing that, we're okay."

"Except, you know, when you kicked me off your property."

A smile lit his face. "Yeah, except then. And when I saved you with my boat. I didn't say you weren't a pain in my ass."

She laughed, then they grew quiet again. She was thinking about how their friendship had evolved when her stomach growled loudly in the silence.

"Someone is hungry."

"I have eggs and sourdough bread. Maybe even some bacon. You want breakfast?"

"I would. But it means not sneaking away before Jeremy has a chance to see my car."

She pushed away and rested on her elbows so she could see him better. "That would bother you, huh."

"Him knowing? Not that, exactly. It's more the questions to follow." He lifted an eyebrow. "I hate when people want me to explain myself."

"I have an answer for that."

"Do tell."

She grinned. "Practice saying this phrase— *It's none of your business.*"

Bran's face straightened into a serious expression. "It's none of your business."

"Nope. Not convinced. Try again."

This time it was accompanied by an angled eyebrow. "It's none of your business."

"Better. Let's practice some more. Hey, Bran, how's the new novel coming?"

He grinned. "It's none of your business."

"What's it about? Come on, you can tell me that."

Firmer this time: "It's none of your business."

"Good! And wow. You spent the night with Jess. Are you sure that was a good thing?"

He rolled slightly and placed a kiss on her naked shoulder. "Oh, I'm very sure it was a good thing," he replied, his voice husky.

"Tsk-tsk. That's not the right answer."

"Yes, it is," he murmured, running his fingers through her hair. "But it's none of Jeremy's business, or Tori's either." He kissed her, long and slow, and then slid out from beneath the covers and left the bedroom, presumably heading toward the dryer and his clothes.

Her body was still humming from the power of that kiss, though. He was very, very good at it.

She slipped out from beneath the sheets and pulled on underwear and last night's yoga pants and top. She'd shower later, before she had to make the trip to Halifax to pick up more supplies.

Branson was in the kitchen, already boiling water for making coffee in her French press, his shorts and T-shirt wrinkled from being in the dryer overnight, but looking entirely scrumptious. She let him work his magic—clearly he knew his way around coffee—and dug out eggs, and bacon she bought at the farmer's market. She put the latter to fry in a cast iron pan, then set to work slicing sourdough bread for toast.

The scent of bacon and coffee filled the air and she smiled up at Bran, who'd found her mugs and had poured her a cup of coffee. It was nice having him here, though it played havoc with her heart a little. She was not sticking around. It wouldn't be good to get used to this kind of domestic scene, would it?

Bran took over toasting the bread while Jess drained the bacon and then cracked eggs into the pan. "How do you like your eggs? Over? Yolks hard or soft?"

"Over and just set."

Just like she preferred hers.

Soon they were seated at her tiny table, with bacon, eggs, and pots of butter and jam between them for the toast. "Delicious," Bran said, chewing on a strip of bacon.

"Big breakfast is one of my favorites," she admitted. "Sometimes I even like having breakfast for dinner."

He laughed. "Me, too. Only with pancakes."

"Mmm… Or waffles."

She spread raspberry jam on her toast and took a bite. "So. What's on your agenda for today?"

He shrugged. "Changing my clothes. Going over some of the stuff from yesterday, with the restoration and stuff. You?"

"Actually, I think I'm the one heading to Halifax today. I want to visit a shop there for more supplies. I've only been there once since arriving. To be honest, I could stand a little city life for a day. As much as I love all this nature, I miss people sometimes. The vitality of it."

Bran was quiet for a moment, took a sip of his coffee, then looked her in the eye. "What if I went with you? We could make a day of it. You could pick up your supplies, and we could go for dinner someplace nice downtown."

"Like a date?"

Again, he shrugged. "If you want to call it that. We could just call it hanging out."

It did sound lovely. A couple of hours drive on a beautiful summer day, an errand or two, and then a fine dinner… She hadn't done that in a long time. Especially with company. She'd spent the last several months traveling alone, and she'd enjoyed it, but she couldn't deny it was a lonely existence.

"You're welcome to come along."

"Do you want me to drive, or take yours?" He lifted an eyebrow. "If we take mine, you can have some wine with dinner. I'm happy to be your designated driver."

It was a generous offer, but she already felt a little odd, considering he wasn't drinking at all. "I don't need wine," she said, popping the last crust of toast into her mouth.

"You say that, but the place I have in mind has a very good wine list. And it doesn't bother me, Jess. Truly."

She took his plate and stacked it on her own. "Then I accept. It sounds like a very nice day, and since my cooking is plain at best, a dinner out sounds lovely."

"Perfect." He pushed away from the table and then checked his watch. "It's nearly eight. Jeremy will have noticed my car by now. Time to answer the inevitable questions, and head home for a shower. What time should I pick you up?"

She pondered for a moment. "Eleven? It would give me a couple of hours to work before we go."

"Sounds perfect."

She took the dishes to the sink, and when she turned back again, there was an odd moment where they stood and stared at each other.

"Okay. So the awkward exit is a thing," he said, then took a step forward and kissed her on the cheek. "Thanks for last night," he murmured, his lips close to her ear. "I'll see you in a few hours."

She nodded, feeling a little breathless.

And then he was gone.

Jess stared at the door for ten seconds, then shook herself into action. First, work. Then, a shower.

And then, the rest of the day with a man who could never really be hers.

CHAPTER EIGHT

BRAN RETURNED AT just past eleven o'clock. He'd left without encountering Jeremy, nor was there any questioning text message from either him or Tori. They either hadn't noticed his car, or they were minding their own business. If he were a betting man, he'd say they had slept in and missed his exit. Because Jeremy wouldn't hesitate to put in his two cents.

This time, instead of parking in the main driveway, he pulled in next to Jess's car. She came outside and shut the door behind her, and his breath caught a little.

He wasn't supposed to be feeling this way. Not now. Maybe not ever. And yet he wasn't going to cancel their plans. It was just a summer thing. He wasn't going to fall in love, so that wasn't an issue. And they were both clear on that, weren't they? She was leaving to go back to Chicago. Why shouldn't they combat some of their loneliness with each other?

Jess wore a pretty little dress with a light blue background and tiny pink flowers, with cute little blue sandals on her feet. She looked as fresh and pretty as a spring morning, with her sunny hair shining and grazing the tips of her shoulders in soft waves. A bag was slung over her shoulder, a pastel-colored tapestry kind of thing that suited her completely. "Have you been waiting?" she asked, descending the two steps to the graveled walk.

"Only for a few minutes. You look very nice." He moved to the passenger side to open her door. Lord, she smelled delicious, too. Like sweet peas softened by hints of vanilla.

"Thanks." She smiled up at him. "No paint-stained jeans and tees for me today. If we're going to dinner, I wanted to dress up a little."

She looked him up and down too, as he held open the door. "You also look very nice."

He needed a haircut, but there hadn't been time. But he'd trimmed his beard and put aside jeans and tees for dress pants and a button-down shirt in off-white.

"Well, let's hit the road," he suggested, and watched the long length of her leg as she slid into the car and he shut the door behind her.

They drove to Halifax in just under two hours. The highway traffic was light, and they only hit one small section of construction. Bran used the car's GPS to navigate his way to the art supply store Jess had picked, and went inside with her as she browsed and made her purchases. They stowed everything in his trunk, and then he suggested a walk in the popular public gardens.

The sun was bright, and there was a light breeze as they made their way to the entrance. "It's a beautiful day," she said, letting out a happy sigh. "This was such a good idea, Bran."

"The gardens will be packed, but I hear they're beautiful. If you like flowers."

She patted her bag. "I'll make a confession. I brought a small sketch pad with me."

He laughed. Laughing was so easy with her, particularly when she looked up at him with a twinkle in her eye. "Of course you did."

"Don't tell me you don't always have a notebook with you."

He angled a wry look in her direction. "Of course I don't." Then after a moment, he added, "I voice record on my phone."

But he wasn't interested in dictating now. He just wanted to spend the afternoon with her, in the early summer sun, and live in the moment.

It was miles better than living in the past.

The garden was heavy with tourists and what appeared to be a couple of bus tour groups. As they entered the ornate iron gates, a strange amphibious vehicle approached the intersection, loaded with tourists and a guide narrating local history. They sent up a strange cry of "ribbit-ribbit" as they passed, and then Bran chuckled. "The Harbor Hopper," he said, nudging her and pointing. "Want to go? From the look of it, it's one of those land and sea tour things."

"Oh, my," she replied, laughing as the vehicle pulled away, the guide changing topic. "I'm not sure I'm dressed for that."

"I'm sure you wouldn't fall in." He took her hand in his. "But if you did, I'm a strong swimmer."

"One ocean rescue is enough for me." She pushed up her sunglasses. "Oh, Bran. You were right, this is gorgeous."

They wandered along the paths, meandering slowly around all the different flower beds, examining species of tree and shrub and bloom. Couples posed for pictures and selfies on a small stone bridge, and Jess kindly offered to snap photos of a couple on their honeymoon. The smell was absolutely heavenly: fresh-cut grass and the heavy, sweet scent of lilacs; rhododendrons in various shades of purple, the size of cars, were in full, showy bloom, and the annual flower beds offered bright rainbows of colors. They ambled in the shade and stopped for Jess to take out her pencils and sketch a la-

burnum tree, the yellow chains of flowers re-
minding Bran of a sunshine-hued wisteria.

They stopped again and sat on a bench near
the pond. A middle-aged man fed the ducks
on the bank, and Bran was happy to sit and
watch as Jess worked away, her pencil strokes
brisk and confident. A tiny replica of the *Titanic* floated on the water, and Bran considered
telling Jess the city's connection to the disaster,
only he didn't want to interrupt her.

She was in another world when she sketched.
Her focus was razor sharp, and nothing escaped
her notice as her gaze darted between subject
and paper.

He was happy to people watch. He leaned
back on the bench, crossed an ankle over his
knee, and watched the dynamics between parents and children, old and young, couples on
dates and those who seemed to have been together for a long time. They were the ones
who didn't have to hold hands to show intimacy; it was in their relaxed body language
and the easy way they touched each other in
passing, speaking of a comfort and devotion
that pricked at Bran's capricious contentment.
Strangers wandered together, name tags stuck
to their shirts from some sort of guided tour.
They were smiling and polite as they talked to

each other, pointing out blossoms and reading the species signs dotted throughout the garden.

A father and son left the pathway nearby, the boy holding his dad's hand as they picked their way over the grass toward a handful of ducks near the water's edge. "Dada, ducks!" the boy exclaimed. Bran guessed he was maybe three. He swallowed thickly. Owen would be about the same age now, if he were alive. Would he have liked ducks? Held Bran's hand, maybe in Central Park on Saturdays?

Watching the two of them play by the water, the way the father patiently kept the boy from the edge, or pointed out all the different colored feathers from each species, warmed his heart. The ache was bittersweet; he was sure he would never quite get over losing his child. But it hurt less today.

Jess looked over at him, put her hand on his knee. "They're sweet, aren't they?"

He nodded, unable to tear his eyes away. "He's a good dad."

"You can have it again someday, you know," she offered gently. "When you're ready."

Bran tore himself away from the father and son scene and met her gaze. "No," he said quietly. "I can't. I can't go through that again. But I'm getting to a place where I'm okay with it."

"Then maybe you'll get to a place where you'll consider it again, too. You never know."

But he shook his head. "No," he repeated. "I know. I had my shot at a family, and I won't chance going through this hell again."

The pink in her cheeks deepened. "I'm sorry," she murmured. "I didn't mean to press."

"You didn't. It's just…there's not much I'm sure of. But that's one thing I am. And I've made my peace with it."

The father and son had moved on, skirting the pond. And Bran got up from the bench, ready to move on, as well.

Jess shoved her sketch pad into her bag and hurried to catch up with Bran, who was starting down the path toward the middle of the gardens. She hadn't meant to upset him, but clearly she had. She should have known better than to bring up fatherhood. It was still too raw for him. At the same time, she'd never been more sure that their relationship was destined for a dead end. He really didn't want a family again, and she did. Being with him, and being around the Fishers had shown her that she did want children of her own. And a partner to share life with. And yet something held her back from saying the words out loud. She could tell Bran all about life not giving guarantees, but she also understood why a person wouldn't want to set themselves up for potential heartbreak.

After all, she'd been doing it for years.

And still there was Bran to consider. It would be easier to end things right now. Probably smarter, too. But she didn't want to. Not yet.

"Hey, wait up," she called, trotting to catch up to him. When she did, she took a deep breath and matched her steps to his. "You gonna be okay?"

He nodded. "Yeah. I'm okay."

"I overstepped, Bran. I really am sorry."

He reached down for her hand, a reassuring gesture that touched her heart. "I know you are. And don't worry about pressing me. It's good for me. It helps, even when it makes me grumpy."

Forgiven, she kept her hand in his as they made their way to the large gazebo that was the centerpiece of the gardens. People milled around, and there was a line at a small building to their left, which appeared to house public bathrooms and a small café, complete with ice cream. The large patio area was full of people enjoying the sweet, cold treat. "You want some?" Bran asked.

"Do you?" She wasn't really hungry, even though they hadn't had lunch. The big breakfast had been super filling, but could she really pass up ice cream in the park?

"A small one? It looks delicious."

They detoured into the building and waited in line for the hand-paddled treat. When they got to the front of the line, she chose blueberries and cream for her flavor. Bran went for a more sedate maple walnut, and then they emerged out into the bright sunshine again.

"Let's find a place to sit," he suggested. "Someplace with shade. I don't want to be responsible for you getting a sunburn."

She was sure the sun had already left a bit of a burn on her shoulders. Her pale complexion meant she burned easily, and she hadn't thought to bring sunscreen today. "How about up there?" She pointed to the top end of the garden, where there was an open area bordered by benches and leafy trees. There was even a chess table adding character to the area.

"Perfect."

Her ice cream was starting to melt by the time they got to the benches, and they picked one that was shaded and would remain so as the sun shifted. For several minutes they ate in comfortable silence. Despite the earlier tension, Jess couldn't remember the last time she'd been so comfortable with someone. They didn't need to talk. Didn't need to fill up the space with empty words that meant nothing. She finished her ice cream, and he finished his, and he took their garbage to a nearby trash can. When he came back, he put his arm along the back of the bench, and she relaxed against him, her head resting in the curve of his shoulder.

"People watching," he said softly. "I love people watching."

"Ana and I used to make up stories about people," she offered, a smile touching her lips. "Like that woman there." She nodded toward a woman several yards away, sitting on an identical bench and reading. "What's her story, do you think?"

Bran tapped a finger to his lips. "She's waiting for someone, but he's late. He's always late, so she brings a book so she doesn't look as if she's waiting."

"Well, that's sad. Why does she have to be waiting for a man, anyway?" She lifted her eyebrows. "I think she's single. Maybe she's just broken up with someone because she wants to be put first. So she's putting herself first and spending an afternoon exactly how she wants—in the gardens in the sunshine and with a good book."

"The heroine of her own life."

"You bet." She grinned up at him. "Do you always go for the sad and tragic?"

"Waiting for someone isn't exactly tragic."

"I don't know. Waiting for someone who is chronically late and doesn't care enough to show up on time… I mean, if someone loves you, they should be impatient. Like they can't wait for that moment when they see you again. A thirst that needs to be quenched."

He laughed and squeezed her shoulder a little. "Are you sure you're not a writer?"

"I'm an observer," she answered. "Okay, tell me another one."

He looked around for a moment, then nodded. "That old gentleman there." The man in question was walking slowly along the path with the aid of a cane. A cap shielded his eyes, and he wore a long-sleeved shirt and pants even though the day was hot. "He comes here every day to walk. He used to come here with his wife, but she's no longer with him. But it doesn't matter to him. He's not sad. He walks and he remembers, and he's thankful for the years they had together. And when he gets home to his little apartment, he tells her picture about everything he saw. Because she's still with him."

She loved the wistful picture he drew with words. "You're a romantic, Branson Black. Don't deny it."

He shrugged. "I suppose I can be. When

I'm not murdering people and creating horrible villains."

"Everyone has a little darkness inside them. It's all about the choices."

He was quiet for a few moments.

"I saw the darkness for a while, Jess. I'm not gonna lie."

"I know, sweetheart. I know."

"It's not so dark lately, though. I have you to thank for that."

Her heart warmed, and a tingly sensation wound its way from her chest down to her belly. Sometimes she wished she didn't have this visceral reaction to him, and other times she reveled in it. Today he'd made it clear that he wasn't interested in anything serious, wasn't looking to have more children or a family. Where did that leave her? She wanted those things. Maybe not right this minute, but eventually. Hoping for him to change was a sure path to disappointment. This summer—these few weeks—were all they would have together. She wanted to cherish them, but to do so she had to remind herself that she could not fall in love with him, and she had to live in the moment.

Could she do that? Because if she couldn't, she should walk away right now.

She looked up at him. He'd closed his eyes

and lifted his face to the sun that filtered through the leafy canopy.

As if he could sense her gaze, he said, "You should sketch. You know you want to."

She did, so she leaned forward and retrieved her sketch pad. But it wasn't flowers or trees or strangers that she drew. It was him, and the angle of his jaw, the crisp edges of his lips, his soft eyelashes, and the way his unruly hair touched his shoulders when his head was tipped back.

She wasn't in love, but she wouldn't lie and say her heart wasn't involved. Of course it was. Her pencil moved quickly across the paper, then she reached for another with a softer lead. She wanted to capture the unguarded moment as best she could before he opened his eyes and caught her.

The sketch was rough but there was something in it she liked. It wasn't perfect, but the sweeping strokes captured an urgency and energy that surprised her.

Bran opened his eyes, squinting and looking at her. She turned the page over and smiled up at him, hoping he hadn't seen the sketch. She wanted it just for her.

She wanted to have something to remember him by when their time together was over.

As, of course, it would be.

CHAPTER NINE

HE TOOK HER to dinner at a seafood restaurant in the city's downtown core. While she went for a seafood pasta, he ordered steak and an appetizer of mussels in a garlic cream sauce. Best of all was the history of the place, which had its beginnings as a school, then as a mortuary, particularly during the time of the *Titanic* sinking and a massive explosion that had leveled the north end during the First World War. Jess listened raptly as Bran told her what he knew of the place, and then grinned when he said it was haunted.

"Do you really believe in that stuff?" she asked, taking a sip of the fine semi-dry white she'd ordered.

"Of course I do. Don't you?"

She shrugged. "I don't know. I mean, I think it's possible. I just haven't experienced anything that would, you know, make me really believe."

After a moment of hesitation, she looked

up at him. "Have you ever, you know, seen a ghost?"

He furrowed his brow and picked at his potato for a few moments. "No? I mean, not actually seen a ghost. But I've felt things that I can't really explain."

She held her breath as she asked, "You mean Jennie?"

He sighed and met her gaze, his eyes sad. "You know, at times I kind of wish Jennie would show up. I'd like to see her again. And then as soon as I think that, I realize that if she did, it'd scare me to death. I don't know what I'd do. Or say."

And make it harder to let go, Jess thought, but she kept the words locked inside.

They changed the subject and chatted over the magnificent dinner, and even though Jess was stuffed, she agreed to share a serving of lemon tart. It was after eight when they finished and made their way back to his car. It would be ten before they reached home, and just dark, as the days were long. Jess was determined now not to return to the maudlin subject of his wife; it had dampened the mood earlier and while she had no problem being an ear for his thoughts, twice during the day she'd felt as if there was a third person on their date. It seemed Bran was determined, too, because he'd reverted back to his easy manner as he opened the car door for her, and closed it solicitously before getting in on the driver's side. Once behind the wheel, he hesitated, then reached for her hand.

"Thank you for allowing me to tag along today. It was nice, don't you think?"

Yes, it had been nice. Despite the conversation getting heavy at times. She'd enjoyed his company, but something had been missing. So nice was a perfectly adequate word.

"What's wrong?" he asked quietly. He hadn't yet started the car, and the silence around them was heavy.

She shifted in her seat and looked over at him. "Did things get weird today? Are you having regrets?"

His eyes warmed. "No, I'm not. I'm sorry if I got moody. It's just that...well, for a long time, that moodiness was a constant. Lately not so much." He squeezed her fingers. "Lately I've found myself enjoying things. I forget to be sad. So when those moments creep in, I'm not ready for them." He smiled a little. "I think it's a good thing, really. Forgetting to be sad. Maybe someday I actually won't be sad at all."

She squeezed his hand back. "Thank you for telling me," she said softly. "I wondered if I'd done something wrong."

"No, nothing," he assured her, and then leaned over the seat and kissed her gently. "You are lovely and sweet and strong." He kissed her again, and she melted a little, leaning into the soft and seductive contact. "You're just what I need, Jess."

Her heart slammed against her ribs as she opened her mouth and led him to a deeper kiss. Desire darkened the sweetness of it, like rich chocolate over marshmallow. He let go of her hand and threaded his fingers through her hair, and she moaned against his lips as his strong fingers massaged the back of her head.

He pulled away, a little reluctantly, she thought, and stared down at her. "We're in a car in broad daylight," he said, his voice a bit rough. "Put a pin in this until we get home?"

"It's a long drive," she said.

"We could spend the night in the city. Drive back in the morning."

The suggestion came as such a surprise she was temporarily dumbstruck. Finally she managed a weak, "Bran…"

"Order room service for breakfast."

Never in her life had she ever rented a hotel room for sex. And yet the two-hour drive seemed interminably long, and the idea of spending the night in a hotel was exciting. His gaze held hers and the tension in the car leaped.

"Bran," she said, trying for a low note of caution. Instead that single syllable—his name—came out with a breathy sort of yearning. "I think… I want to…"

Oh, dear.

He turned the car on and pulled out of the spot, navigating a few streets until he reached the hotel she'd noticed earlier, across from the gardens. He parked in the underground garage, and without looking at her, got out and came around to open her door.

She grabbed her tote bag while a rush of feelings swept through her body. Excitement. Arousal, for sure. Anxiety. Were they rushing things? Was this really a smart idea?

"Relax," he whispered, taking her hand as they made their way into the hotel and to the front desk. Within moments he'd secured them a room and was guiding her to the elevator.

As they waited for the elevator, Bran took her hand. Jess swallowed against a nervous lump in her throat. Were they really doing this? Last night had been one thing. They'd been in her place, talking and snuggling after a make-out session on the beach. It had seemed…a logical progression of events. This was different. The bell dinged and the doors opened, and Bran guided her inside. She let out a long slow breath and asked herself a sudden question.

What would Ana do?

Jess bit down on her lip. Ana wasn't here. But Ana had lived life until the last moment, and she'd undoubtedly tell Jess to grab what happiness she could while it lasted. Jess chanced a look over at Bran, and he looked back at her, unsmiling, his dark eyes gleaming. None of the intensity in the car had been lost, and she got a thrill seeing the desire in his eyes.

No one was guaranteed another day. Look at Ana. Look at Jennie. You had to grab each day and its precious, fleeting moments.

The doors opened and they stepped out, then hesitated while Bran scanned the plate on the wall with arrows to room numbers.

They were off again, down the hall, stopping in front of a door, waiting while he let them in and shut the door behind them.

Jess had a glimpse of a king-sized bed covered in white and gold linens, and matching draperies on either side of an elegant desk. It was more luxurious than even Bran's room at his house, but the moment after the door shut, the sheer opulence of the room was forgotten. Bran's mouth was on hers, his hands were on her waist and she was swept entirely away into a sea of sensation.

CHAPTER TEN

BRAN WOKE WITH light streaming through the window. He checked the clock beside the bed: five forty. The days were incredibly long at this time of year. Last night, before they'd fallen asleep, sated, it had still been daylight. He'd slept straight through, dreamless. He regretted that he hadn't awakened in the night, simply to make the hours last longer.

Jess was breathing slow and deep beside him, her face turned toward him, her hair strewn on the white linen of the pillowcase. She was so beautiful, with her sunrise-colored hair and delicate lips. An unfamiliar tenderness washed over him. The sex was fantastic, but it was more than that. They were friends.

He wondered if that friendship would be ruined now that they'd slept together. Certainly, after the summer, their relationship would be over. And yet he'd miss her. She understood him in a way that was so…well, easy.

Yes, he was going to miss her.

She shifted and rolled to her right side, so that her back was to him. It was early to wake her, so instead he slid closer, gently putting his arm over her waist and snuggling in, spoon-style. He closed his eyes and drank in the scent of her hair and the light musk of her skin. For two years he'd slept alone. The last two nights he'd had Jess with him, and it would be too easy to get used to her there. Spending time with her was one thing. Having fun was fine. But he wouldn't use her as a tonic for his loneliness, and he wouldn't get too used to her.

Last night had been impulsive and exciting, but they couldn't make a habit of this, could they?

But reality was hours away, and he wanted to absorb every moment he could. So he closed his eyes and imprinted the moment on his memory, until she woke up.

He didn't mean to fall back asleep, but when he opened his eyes again, Jess was facing him with a soft smile on her face.

"Good morning."

"Hi," he answered. Her foot slid along his calf, just a light caress, but it instantly brought his body to attention. "Sleep well?"

"Too well," she laughed. "I think I got more

than a full eight hours. I don't remember the last time that happened."

He wiggled his eyebrows, and she laughed again. Maybe keeping it light was the way to go.

"I think we wore each other out."

She blushed, and he loved it.

A piece of hair had fallen over her cheek, and he reached out and tucked it back behind her ear. "So, what do you think? Room service?"

"Why not?"

"What do you like?"

This time she wiggled her eyebrows, and he laughed. Lord, she was such a ray of sunshine. "Everything," she answered.

His brain took a direct trip back to last night, and his body wasn't far behind. But while they'd been a bit crazed and frantic, he didn't want to assume this morning would be a continuation. As much as he would like it to be. He pushed the thoughts aside as best he could and rolled to the night table, where he grabbed the folder containing the in-room dining guide. A few minutes later he'd ordered a veritable feast, due to be delivered in thirty minutes.

She sat up, the sheets tucked under her arms, covering her breasts. "So…uh…want to shower before breakfast?"

He swallowed tightly. "Together?"

There was that blush again. The air of innocence around her was enchanting. She didn't
need to ask again; they made their way to the
luxurious bathroom and spent five minutes
cleaning up and fifteen finding mind-blowing
pleasure. After they'd caught their breath and
dried with the fluffy towels, they dressed in the
hotel-provided robes and waited for their meal.

When it came, he watched as she loaded her
plate with French toast and fruit and bacon,
then drizzled on enough maple syrup that it
puddled under everything. He liked her so
much. Liked just about everything about her.
But as they shared a laugh over her love of the
syrup, he realized something important.

He didn't love her. Or at least, he wasn't in
love with her. It came as a huge relief. He didn't
want to love again. And they were having fun,
weren't they? A summer fling.

He bit into his omelet and frowned. Jeremy
and Tori had a summer fling and look at them
now. But that wouldn't happen to him. Jess was
on the pill, and so there wouldn't be a surprise
baby popping up. Even so, perhaps he'd be wise
to stop at a pharmacy and grab some condoms
just in case. There was no harm in doubling
up, was there?

"You okay, Bran?" Jess's light voice interrupted his thoughts. "You look like you disappeared for a moment."

"I'm perfect," he replied, feeling on surer ground now. "This is delicious. And so are you."

She blushed and he grinned. "What?" she asked, tilting her head a bit in that adorable way she had.

"You blush a lot, and I like it."

The pink color deepened. "I blush at everything, so there."

"Mmm-hmm." He stood and leaned over the table to get a taste of her maple-sweet lips. "I still like it."

After breakfast they dressed in their clothes from the day before, and Bran dropped the key at the desk before they made their way to the parking garage. In no time, they were back on the highway and headed home. Bran's heart felt lighter than it had in years, and he tapped his fingers on the steering wheel in time to the music playing through the speakers. Jess told him about her agent wanting to set up a showing in the fall, and how much she was enjoying painting again. Truthfully, Bran couldn't wait to get home and open his laptop. He wasn't going to push, but he felt the urge to write, and he wanted to strike while the iron was hot. He'd always been a disciplined writer, working consistently but also riding a wave of inspiration when it hit.

It seemed no time at all that they arrived at Jeremy's, and he parked behind her car at the boathouse. He helped her take in her packages from the art store, and then hesitated on the threshold. "So, I'll see you soon?"

She nodded. "You know where I am." Her smile was sweet. "I'll be here, painting."

"Good." He reached out and pulled her close again, kissing her lightly. "I had a really great time," he murmured against her mouth.

"Me, too."

He left her standing there on the porch, and found himself whistling as he slid behind the wheel of his car and backed out of the lane, heading home once more.

Jess changed out of her dress and into more comfortable clothes—denim capris and a T-shirt—then organized her new supplies and studied the painting she had been working on for a week. She was happy with how it was progressing, and she spent an hour and a half working on it, trying to focus. But something wasn't quite right.

She stepped back and thought for a moment, and then, to her surprise, she rushed forward and removed the canvas from the easel and replaced it with a fresh one.

Something else was calling to her right now. She pulled out the photo of the first day, and then the sketch she'd done, and knew she had to paint it. The one with Bran looking out to sea.

For a moment she rolled her eyes and let out a sigh. Two nights with a man and suddenly he was her subject? And yet, she'd been drawn to that moment time and again over the last few weeks. The loneliness telegraphed in his body language, in the gray sea beyond him and the weary lighthouse. A thread of excitement wound through her as she started the process of turning canvas to art. She forgot the time, forgot to eat, forgot everything but the work until there was a knock on her door.

She checked her watch, shocked to discover it was almost four in the afternoon. She removed her apron as she made her way to the door, and opened it to find Tori on the other side, a frown immediately replaced by a relieved smile as she saw Jess in the doorway.

"Oh, good, you're all right!" Tori slipped into the boathouse, leaving Jess feeling off balance. She'd been so swept up in work that the interruption had her head trying to catch up.

"All right?" she parroted, following Tori into the main room.

"I stopped by yesterday and you didn't answer."

"Oh, is that all?" Jess laughed a little. "I went into Halifax for supplies."

Tori's brow wrinkled. "You did? But your car was here. And I texted, too. Gosh, I hope I got the right number."

Jess felt the heat creep up her neck. She hadn't even checked her phone since yesterday afternoon. She'd been utterly preoccupied—first with Bran and then with work.

"How did you get to Halifax?" Tori asked, and the heat reached Jess's ears.

"Oh, um, Branson had some things to do so we went together. No biggie." She smiled widely. "And it saved me from having to navigate the city. Bran's much more familiar."

Tori's face sobered. "You and Bran, huh?"

Oh, Lordy. She had such a horrible poker face. "Yeah, well, we get along okay now." A memory slid into her brain, of his face in the shower this morning, and she struggled to breathe. "At least he doesn't hate me anymore."

"Oh," Tori said, "no danger of that. He walked you home the other night."

"It's no big deal," Jess replied. And hoped beyond hope that Tori hadn't seen his car yesterday morning.

"Well, I'm hoping Jeremy and I didn't make a mistake." She rested her hand on the countertop. "We kind of pushed you two together, you know? Bran needed someone to shake him up a bit. But…" She peered into Jess's face. "It's more than shaking up, isn't it?"

Jess had to make light of this. She really didn't want Tori to butt in, or start asking more detailed questions. For one, she didn't know how she'd answer. The last two nights had been amazing, but they'd also shaken her more than she wanted to admit.

"I promise you have nothing to feel badly about. I like Bran, he likes me, and sometimes we spend time together without fighting." Indeed. "Really, Tori, it's no big deal."

"So you're just enjoying each other's company?"

Jess let out a relieved breath. "Yes, that's exactly it."

Tori tapped her finger on her lips. "Hmm. Okay. I'm going to shut up now because I don't want to pry too deeply. I just…well, we love Bran, and I like you a lot, Jess. Jeremy and I don't want to see either of you hurt."

The words were heartfelt, so Jess relaxed a little and motioned toward the tiny table and chairs. "Listen, sit down for a bit and let me get you a drink."

Tori did sit, and as Jess went to the fridge, she called out, "So where's Rose this afternoon?"

"Sleeping. Jeremy's home and working in his office, with the baby monitor next to him." Jess turned around and saw Tori smiling. "I love her to bits, but going somewhere, even for thirty minutes, without a baby and the requisite gear is so nice."

"You didn't venture far," Jess teased. "Soda water okay? I have some flavored stuff. Lemon lime or grapefruit."

"Ooh, grapefruit, please," Tori replied. Jess retrieved two cans, opened them and poured them over ice before returning to the table. She sat across from Tori and tried to relax, though she was still feeling odd about the whole thing. She wasn't accountable to anyone, but the night away was still more of a secret than anything, for the simple reason that she wanted to avoid questions.

"You started a new painting," Tori said, staring at the white canvas. "What's this one?"

"Actually, it's from a photo I took the first day. Bran was looking out over the point, and he seemed so lost and lonely. The image hasn't left me alone, so I figure it's time to get started on it."

Tori's voice was soft. "You really care for him, don't you? Oh, Jess. I'm afraid we really did goof. I don't want to see you fall for him, only to get hurt."

The consideration was genuine, and Jess patted Tori's hand. "It's fine. We like each other but neither of us is after anything serious. We've talked about it, Tori, so truly, don't worry. I'm going to paint to my heart's content, and at the end of the summer I'm going to head back home to my life. Besides, Bran is not in a relationship place. He's still too hung up on his wife."

"I never knew her. Jeremy says she was lovely, though, and that they were very happy."

"Hard to compete with that." She took a sip of her soda water. "Not that I want to. Still, we enjoy spending time together. That's all there is."

And the sex, she thought, but didn't say. She and Tori had become friends but weren't quite close enough to be confidants of that sort.

"So you aren't falling in love with him?"

"Of course not."

Jess said the words with confidence, but she knew deep down it wasn't strictly true. No matter how often she repeated the words to herself—summer romance, short-term fling—she couldn't erase the sight of Bran while they were making love, the intense expression on his face as he gazed into her eyes as if no one else existed. He was an extraordinary man, smart and sexy and deep, sometimes grouchy and other times sweet, and a man who knew how to love a woman with all his heart. Of course she was falling for him. Her head was in the clouds, and there was going to be an awful thud at the end. The difference was this time she wasn't going to be blindsided. She saw it coming and could prepare.

And yet, she looked at Tori and said, "Men like Bran don't come along often. I'd be a fool not to spend whatever time I can with him. Even knowing the outcome."

Tori nodded and looked down in her glass, and looked up again, her eyes bright as if she might cry. "I felt the same way about Jeremy." Her voice was soft and dreamy. "And I was fine after he left, mostly. Until he came back. You're right, though. Bran isn't ready for anything serious. As long as you know that, and you're having fun...more power to you."

"I appreciate you caring, Tori, I do. But I've got this."

"Of course you do. You're a strong woman. I think that's why Bran likes you. None of those men are the kind who like pushovers."

"I think that's a compliment."

Tori laughed. "The best kind. Now, I'd better get back up to the house. I truly am glad you're okay. I was worried you'd got sick or something."

"I'm absolutely fine," she replied. "But thank you for caring." At least Tori hadn't realized that Jess hadn't returned home until this morning. The conversation had been personal enough without that information being out in the open.

After Tori left, Jess made an early dinner since she'd missed lunch. She checked her email on her phone; no texts from Bran. That was okay. After the past forty-eight hours, maybe he needed time to process everything. She certainly did.

Because she was falling for him, no question. But he didn't need to know that. And neither did Tori.

CHAPTER ELEVEN

BRAN LOOKED UP from his laptop and squinted. Ever since his return from Halifax, he'd either been embroiled in research, or working on the opening chapters of the new book. It had felt wonderful working again. The words weren't quite flowing, but they were there, ready for him to pluck out of his brain and put them on the page. Now the story had a basic outline, he had pages full of notes and his master document had the better part of two full chapters written.

Not long now, and he'd call his agent and tell him the good news. Maybe send him some pages. But right now, the light was dimming and he'd been working the better part of sixteen hours.

He checked the date on the bottom right corner of the screen. Was that correct? Had he been back from Halifax for three days already? And he hadn't heard from Jess. Not once. Nor had he texted.

He hit the save button and slumped back in his chair. He wasn't sure what to do about Jess, really. To say he wanted her was an understatement. Having sex again had been amazing... she was a good lover, sweet and generous and passionate. Their nights together had been wonderful, but he'd stayed quiet for two reasons. One, he'd gotten the bug to write and he wanted to catch the words while they were there, no longer out of reach. And two, it would be very easy to get wrapped up in her. Spending a few days regaining his equilibrium seemed like a good idea, especially after their dash to the hotel. That wasn't his usual style. There was a "can't keep my hands off her" edge to his feelings, and it was strange.

She was different from Jennie, and he was so glad. He still hadn't forgotten the way she'd asked if he'd been thinking of his wife when he'd kissed her. He wasn't into looking for a substitute. That wouldn't be fair to Jess, or to him.

But she hadn't called him, either. And that made him wonder if she was having second thoughts.

It wasn't something he wanted to talk about over the phone, so he closed his laptop, changed his shirt and drove over to the boathouse.

The porch light was off, but light poured

from the windows onto the stone path leading to her door. It was nine at night; was she up working this late? Perhaps she'd been painting just as much as he'd been writing.

Then the sound of laughter filtered out through the open window, and he hesitated. She had company?

Maybe he should do this another time.

He hesitated for a full ten seconds, then he heard Tori's laugh and Jeremy's low voice, and then another round of laughter. Something unfamiliar swept over him, and he realized it was loneliness. Not the welcome, self-imposed kind he'd reveled in for the last few years, but the kind that longed to be a part of something warm and fun. Before he could change his mind, he stepped up onto the porch and knocked on the door.

Jess answered, her face alight with laughter as she stood with the door open. "Well, hello, stranger."

"Hi," he said quietly, a little off balance by how happy he was to see her face. It had been what, three days? And he'd missed her terribly.

"Come in. Jer and Tori are here. And little Rose is asleep."

In that much noise? He wasn't sure how it was possible. Owen had always awakened at anything over normal speaking level.

He stepped inside and took off his sandals, padding to the kitchen in his bare feet. Jeremy and Tori were sitting at the round table, with cards in their hands.

"We're playing cribbage," Jess explained. "Tori taught us how. Jeremy is about to get skunked."

He had never played the game in his life, and stared at the oddly shaped board with different colored pegs in various spots. "Oh."

"We're almost done this game," Tori said, taking a sip of what appeared to be sparkling water. "Come on in and watch the carnage."

"There's sparkling water and ginger ale in the fridge. Help yourself, Bran. And chips on the counter."

The small gathering was very different from social occasions he'd gone to as a member of the Black family. No one ever helped themselves, or sat as an odd man out during a game of cards while munching on chips straight from the bag. Instead, it reminded him of days spent at Merrick, playing poker with the guys, drinking contraband beer and pooling snacks.

He'd loved those days. Missed them.

So he helped himself to a ginger ale and grabbed the bag of chips and pulled up a fourth chair to watch. Tori deftly dealt five cards to each player and put one on the table, though he wasn't sure what it was for. Then each of them studied their cards and removed one from their hand, adding it to one on the table.

"All right. Jess, your go."

Branson didn't ask questions, just watched as they took turns laying cards and occasionally moved their pegs on the board. Jess's brow wrinkled each time she considered her play, and he thought she looked adorable. Jeremy sat back in his chair in an indolent posture, very reminiscent of his body language in school. And Tori sat straight and kept an easy expression on her face. He bet she'd be good at poker.

When all the cards had been played, they counted points in some weird format that had something to do with fifteens and runs. Jess had a dozen points, putting her within a few of Tori. There was laughter when Jeremy had four points, keeping him short of the line that had an S beside it. And Tori moved only six. Apparently the four extra cards were hers, too, but to Jess and Jeremy's glee, contained no points.

"One more hand," Jess said, "and this time the crib is mine."

He grabbed a handful of chips and watched.

Jeremy laid a seven after Jess, which gave him two points, putting him one shy of the skunk line. Another round he announced "thirty-one for two" and it put him over, which caused a victorious whoop. "What happens if he doesn't cross?" Bran asked.

"You lose double," Tori replied, grinning. "You just snuck over, Jer."

They continued. Jess played a card and gave a yelp of triumph as she moved three points, so close to Tori and ever closer to the final hole on the board.

At that moment the sound of a baby crying interrupted the game. Jess frowned. "Darn, I'm sorry. I think I woke her."

"It's all right. She'll be fine until we finish this hand."

But Bran looked at Tori and noticed that her relaxed face now had the shadow of tension around her eyes. Tori played a card, and then it was Jess's turn; Rose's crying got louder.

"We can pause the game," Jeremy said. "It's no big deal."

Bran tamped down the apprehension building in his chest and stood. "You guys finish. You're nearly done. I'll go get her."

He walked to the bedroom with heavy steps, totally unsure of himself but knowing he needed to do this sometime. Rose was two months old and he had yet to hold her, even though Jeremy and Tori had named him her godfather. The cries reminded him of a little lamb, bleating with distress. After taking a deep breath, he stepped into the room, went to the bed and scooped her up from the pillow barrier that Tori had set up, even though Rose was nowhere near old enough to roll over yet.

The moment he cradled her against his chest, her cries changed to whimpers. She was so tiny and warm, and he could hear her sucking on her fist as he tucked the light blanket close around her. She smelled like baby lotion and the combination of milk and diapers, and the familiarity of it snuck in and pierced his heart. But there was more than pain there now. There was emptiness but also something more, something warm and glowing that crept in around the corners. Memories that were bitter but also sweet. Her soft, downy head nuzzled into his neck and his throat closed with emotion, tears stinging the backs of his eyes.

"Hello, Rosie. I'm your godfather." He kept his voice low and soothing, and he rocked back and forth a bit as he used to with Owen when he'd been fussy. The cranky noises eased into something that was half-slurp and half-coo, and he closed his eyes and rested his cheek against her.

"You want your mama, huh? Let's go find her."

He reentered the kitchen, and the room suddenly quieted at the sight of him with the baby in his arms. Cards were forgotten in hands as Jeremy's eyes widened and Tori...ah, damn, Tori gave an emotional sniff, and he found his own emotions raw and hovering right at the surface.

Then Jess was there, getting up from her chair and pasting on a smile. "Oh, there's my girl! Look at her all sleepy and snuggly." She went to Bran and didn't take Rose from him, but put her hand on the baby's back. "Tori, do you want me to change her?"

Jess's interference seemed to jolt the others into action, and Tori put down her cards. "Oh, sure, that'd be great! I can get a bottle ready while you do that. Thanks, Jess."

"It's okay. I know where your bag is."

She retrieved a diaper and wipes from the diaper bag in the kitchen, and then motioned for him to follow. He did, following her into the bedroom, where she put down a soft flannel blanket and then took Rose from his arms.

"Unless you want to do the honors?" she asked.

"I, uh…"

She looked up at him, a blinking Rose in her arms. "Baby steps?"

He nodded, unable to say anything more. But he watched as she deftly undid Rose's soft pajamas, changed her diaper and dressed her again, talking softly to the baby the whole time.

"You're very good with her," he observed, his emotions once again riding very close to the surface.

"I like babies." She picked up Rose and set her on her arm. "Isn't that right, sweetie?" And then she met Bran's eyes. "I'd like to have my own someday. But that option hasn't really presented itself. And I'm not at the point where I'm prepared to take things into my own hands."

"You'd like a family, then."

She nodded. "I would. Figuring out how that would fit into my life is another story."

With Rose tidied and dressed, there was no reason to linger, and Jess headed back to the kitchen. But Bran hesitated a moment.

She wanted a family. Babies of her own. If he'd ever thought that this could work between them at all, the idea just died a quick death. He never wanted to do that again. No matter how sweet Rose was. Or how adorable Jess's children would be, with their sunrise hair and blue-green eyes, and a healthy dose of freckles.

Back in the kitchen, he watched while Jess, Jeremy and Tori played out their final hand. Jeremy was over the skunk line, and Jess gave Tori a run for her money, but Tori won by three small points. Rose was in Tori's arms, the bottle braced up so she could eat, and Jeremy pegged the last points for his wife.

"Well," Tori said, sitting back. "That was fun. You're a fast learner, Jess."

"You're a good teacher. Another drink? Anyone want more snacks?"

"We should probably be going," Jeremy said, looking at Bran briefly.

Bran wanted to say that there was no need, that he hadn't come for a specific reason, but the truth was, he had. To test the waters, so to speak. Hoping that Jess's silence wasn't her being angry at him. That she'd been just as busy as he had.

"Yes, and once Rose is fed, she'll go back to sleep. If I can put her in her crib for the night, I might get some good sleep, too."

"Or, you know. Pay attention to your husband."

"Or that." Her grin was teasing but their gazes held, and Bran knew that look. They were so in love. Despite having a baby, they were still in the stage of not getting enough of each other.

He looked at Jess, whose cheeks had gone pink as she picked up dirty glasses from the table.

A few minutes later, Tori and Jeremy said their goodbyes and the house was quiet again. Bran cleared his throat. "I'm sorry I interrupted tonight. I should have called first."

Jess put the glasses in the small dishwasher and shrugged. "It's fine. We were just playing some cards. Tori hasn't gotten out a lot since Rose was born, and doesn't want to leave her with a sitter yet. I think Jeremy was getting a little worried."

She closed the dishwasher and turned to face him. "Was Jennie like that? How old was Owen before you got a sitter?"

He frowned and turned away. "Don't ask me things like that."

But she stepped forward. "Was tonight the first time you held Rose?"

"Jess. Stop." His voice was firm. "I didn't come over to talk about babies, okay? I just... I realized that it's been three days and I didn't call, and I was feeling like a heel about it."

She stopped and stared at him, angling her head a bit as if trying to puzzle him out. "I didn't call you, either."

"Why?"

She looked over at her small living room and then back at him. "To be honest, I needed some time to think. And I've been painting. A lot."

He let out a breath and some of the tension tightening his body. "I've been writing, too."

"I guess our trip was inspiring." Her eyes lit with a bit of the fire he loved, and he was transported back to the hotel room. The way she looked, tasted, sounded.

"So..."

"So I'm not the kind of woman who has to be called hours after being dropped off. I'm not that insecure, Bran. And we both agreed this is not...a real relationship. We want different things. Besides, I have no claim on you or your time. I told myself I was just going to enjoy what time we had."

Her words should have made him feel better, as they essentially let him off the hook. But somehow they didn't, and he couldn't pinpoint why.

"Had," he said quietly. "Past tense?"

"That's up to you." She moved forward. "It got to be too much for you, didn't it?"

"I don't know." He paused and ran his hand through his hair. "It's just a lot. I'm dealing with a lot. You're the first woman I've been with since Jennie. And yeah, tonight was the first time I've held Rose. I'm moving back into the world of the living, but it's hard. I'm not sure I have it in me to navigate...nuance. With a relationship."

She nodded as if she understood completely, but how could she?

"Would it help if we set ground rules?"

He gestured to the small table and chairs.

"Can we sit to discuss this? I feel weird standing here, as if we're facing off."

She obliged him by taking a seat, but angled her chair so that their knees bumped slightly. It helped that she was touching him, actually. Like an anchor to keep him grounded, when he could very easily be overwhelmed.

He could still smell the scent of baby, and his brain remembered a past life he couldn't access anymore. And never would again.

If anything, the past month had taught him that he could move forward without them.

"We both agreed this is a summer thing. That I'll be going back to Chicago and my own life, and you'll be here or wherever else you call home." She folded her hands in her lap. "And since we really do like each other, I think we also agree that there might be a little bit of fear that we'll get too attached to each other."

"Like?" He lifted an eyebrow.

She smiled gently. "Okay, more than like. I care about you, Bran, and I think you care about me. And neither of us wants to get hurt, or be responsible for hurting the other person."

"True."

"So, ground rules. I'll go first. No more overnights."

He blinked. He'd thought she was going to say no sex, but she'd said no staying over. He nodded, thinking of how the intimacy of waking up together made things so much more complicated. "Agreed." Then he added a condition of his own. "No declarations."

"Declarations?"

Bran wasn't sure how to word this one. "I mean, we care about each other. But we both agree that this isn't going to turn into love. I'm not ready for that and like you said, we want different things. So no declarations of love."

"Absolutely. No danger there."

It made him pause for a moment, how quickly she'd said "no danger there." Again, he knew he should be relieved, so why was there this nagging feeling that something was off?

He pushed the feeling aside and ticked off another one on his fingers. "Space to create, and no getting upset when either of us is unavailable because we're working."

She grinned at him. "That's an easy one."

"Maybe. But not for a lot of people. Not everyone gets it."

"Canceling plans is fine, but the courtesy of a call is nonnegotiable. That's just being polite."

"Deal. Or at least… I'll try. I've been known to lose track of time. Anything else?"

She studied him for a long moment. "We agree that we can add to the ground rules as needed if and when things come up we didn't think of tonight."

It was odd, setting rules for something as simple as a casual relationship, but Bran also knew that setting the rules now meant their relationship would stay casual, which was what he wanted. What they both wanted.

He let out a sigh. "Does this feel weird to you?"

And then she laughed, that light, musical sound that he enjoyed so very much, and he smiled, too. The awkwardness and tension of the evening fell away, and she leaned forward, putting her hand over his. "Of course it does. But we both feel the need to protect ourselves, and Bran, I needed to be honest. The only way this is going to work is if we're honest with each other."

Something undefinable flickered behind her eyes, and he briefly wondered what it was, but then she got up from her chair and went to stand in front of him. "And now," she whispered, "will you please kiss me? Because I've been dying for you to for over an hour."

CHAPTER TWELVE

SETTING GROUND RULES seemed to be working. Jess was an early bird, so she was up early each morning, sketching and painting, and usually touched base with Bran when she broke for lunch. Some days they'd venture into the nearby town for errands; sometimes she drove to his house and they spent the day on the beach below his low cliffs, dipping into the ocean and soaking in the sun.

They made love on a blanket in the sand, and in his enormous bed. One evening there was a thunderstorm and the power went out, and so they gathered all the candles he had and put them around the bedroom, making love to the sound of the rain.

She loved his house. Even though it was big, it wasn't cold. No expense had been spared, and sometimes they cooked dinner together in his vast kitchen, which was much better equipped than the boathouse. One afternoon he wrote in

his den, and she pulled a book out of his book-
cases and read. And because that first day she'd
mentioned the Jacuzzi, she arrived one evening
to find a bath drawn and a glass of wine waiting from the bottle she'd gifted him, so she
could soak and watch the ocean through the
windows. It had felt incredibly extravagant and
surreal. Even more surreal when he'd held her
towel when she got out…

But she didn't stay over, and he didn't stay
at the boathouse, either.

It should have been absolutely perfect.

Bran and Jeremy's friend Cole came to town
and stayed at Bran's, which put a bit of a kink
into their social plans. And yet Jess thought it
lovely when she saw the two of them together.
Cole was tall and fair, with a magnetic per-
sonality and an energy that was contagious—
something that had a positive effect on Bran.
He smiled more and laughed often, and Jess
got a glimpse of the man he used to be. She already thought him pretty amazing. But this…it
was different. For a little while, it seemed as if
the weight of the world was off his shoulders,
particularly when he, Cole and Jeremy were all
together. She remembered what he'd said—that
they were family.

Today they were all going to an island off-
shore to look at property. The whole island, in

fact, with the exception of ten acres that was owned by someone else. Cole was considering buying it and turning the mansion into a corporate retreat that he could use for business. Jess tried not to be awestruck when she realized that she was accompanying three billionaires on a shopping spree worth what they were calling a steal—nearly seven million dollars.

The five of them were making a day of it, or at least the better part of a day. Tori's mother was coming to stay with the baby, and it was Tori's first day away from Rose for more than an hour. As she and Bran met the others at the wharf, Jess could tell that Tori was both excited to be going along, and anxious about leaving Rose. She put an arm around Tori's shoulders and gave her a squeeze. "It'll be all right, Mama," she said with a smile. "Grandmas need a chance to spoil babies anyway."

Tori smiled back. "I know. It's just first time nerves. I've got to do it sometime."

Cole had rented a boat for his stay, a fast and luxurious Boston Whaler docked at a nearby marina. The island itself wasn't far outside the bay, but it was only accessible by boat or, Cole explained, by the helipad on-site. Tori looked at Jess and shook her head. Neither of them was used to such luxury, and Jess grinned up at Bran as he sat beside her. "Helipad, huh? Does Cole have his own helicopter?"

Bran shook his head. "Naw. He just charters when he needs to."

Jess's and Bran's definition of *need* seemed to vary, but today she didn't care. Today she was free and ready for fun. How often did one get to visit a private island, anyway?

Cole piloted the boat, and it wasn't long before they were at the island. Instead of docking right away, Cole took them all the way around. Jess got a glimpse of an enormous house with well-trimmed grounds sloping toward the water; the west side had more of a rocky shoreline but the east side had a beautiful sandy beach, similar to the one at Jeremy's, and what looked to be white, soft sand like that by the Sandpiper Resort. The dock was at the southern tip of the island. An ancient fishing boat was already docked, as well as a smaller craft.

Jeremy got off first, and held out his hand to help Tori and then Jess, with Bran and Cole following. "The other Realtor will be at the house. But there should be a golf cart up there—" he pointed to a garage-type structure at the top of the path "—that we can use to get to the main house."

Jess followed the direction of his finger and

noticed not only the garage, but a large house behind it. "That's not the main house, is it?"

He shook his head. "Nope. There's about ten acres that's owned by another party. The house is hers. The rest of the island, about eighty acres or so, is what's for sale."

Interesting. Jess hung back and waited for Bran, and together they walked side by side behind the others. "Your friend is seriously going to buy his own island," she said incredulously.

Bran nodded. "Looks like it. He's right. It's a steal. Besides, Cole's changed a lot in the last year. He tries not to show it, but he has."

"How so?"

"He took over his father's businesses when he was only twenty-three. He's accumulated more since, and I've never seen anyone work so hard or play so hard. It caught up with him and while he won't come right out and say so, I think he hit some burnout. He stepped away for a few months."

"He's okay now?" She looked up ahead. Cole was talking energetically with Jeremy and Tori, his hands gesturing wildly. It was impossible to imagine him slowing down, let alone grinding to a full stop.

Bran nodded. "I think so. But this place… it's different. He doesn't want it to simply acquire something new and shiny. He wants to use it to help executives and companies. Corporate retreats. Team building events. That sort of thing. It's not very Cole, but people change when life kicks them in the ass."

"Like it changed you."

"Cole and I grew up in the same world. We wanted for nothing, but that came with heavy expectations. My parents never wanted for me to be a writer. It was a waste of my time, they said. For a kid who supposedly had every privilege, it felt very much like I was in a cage. Until I got to Merrick and found Cole and Jer. So when my life went sideways, it wasn't all my money or status that got me through it. It was those two."

He looked over at her. "You've been kicked, as well. But you know, quite often we're better people for it."

She wondered at that, really. She knew he'd do anything to turn back the clock and redo that night two years ago. But if he also liked the changes that had happened this summer, that was something huge. "Are you happy, Bran?"

They stopped for a moment and he faced her. "I'm happier than I've been in a very long time, and it's unexpected. I have you to thank for that."

He leaned down and placed a gentle kiss on

her lips. She was stunned; while it was no big secret that she and Bran were spending time together, for him to make such a gesture while they were with his friends felt huge.

"Come on," he said. "We need to catch up or we'll miss our ride."

They climbed on the golf cart, squeezing three of them on the bench seat in the back, and Jeremy drove them past the farmhouse and down a long lane, clear to the other side of the island. The land vacillated between green forests and meadows with waving grass and wildflowers, wild and untamed. But before long the landscape turned into landscaped lawns and gardens, and a grand house appeared.

Cole turned around from the front of the cart and grinned. "Twelve thousand square feet. A dozen bedrooms, eight bathrooms, a kitchen that's a chef's dream and hopefully a room I can convert into a boardroom-type meeting room. What do you think?"

Jess grinned. "It's ginormous!" It was more the size of a hotel than a house.

Cole laughed. "I don't do things halfway. Didn't Bran tell you that?"

She nodded, still grinning. "He did."

The Realtor was waiting for them, and Jess and Bran once again brought up the rear as they were taken on a tour of the house. Jess had never been in anything like it, and was absolutely dazzled. There were indeed twelve bedrooms, each beautifully appointed with gleaming wood furniture and expensive linens. The bathrooms had marble counters and gold fixtures; three had Jacuzzi tubs and there was a sauna downstairs, next to the fully equipped exercise room. A theater room with a large projector screen and theater seating made Jess's eyes goggle.

Back upstairs, the Realtor showed them the addition on the back that held an indoor heated pool. The kitchen was huge, with double stainless-steel refrigerators and a large range with spider burners as well as double wall ovens. There was a small dining area, and then a large adjoining room with a table for at least twelve. To go with the bedrooms, Jess supposed.

One of the large rooms off the foyer could be turned into the meeting room Cole wanted. The other had a conversation pit, and a grand piano in front of tall, gleaming windows.

It was easy to see that Cole was in love with the place, and he and Jeremy kept their heads together, discussing details. Tori took out her phone and called home to check on Rose, and Bran caught Jess's eye and pointed outside. "Come on," he said quietly. "Let's explore outside."

"I'd like that."

The sun was bright and cheery as they stepped out of the grand house. "Oh, it's amazing," she said, "but too big for me."

"I know. But for what he's intending to do with it? It's perfect."

"Probably." She peered up at him. "I think for me it's…not really a home. It doesn't have that homey kind of feeling about it."

Bran studied her for a moment. "Do you feel that way about my house?"

She took his hand, and they started to walk across the plush lawn. "Not really. Yours is different. With yours, it *can* be cozy and welcoming and have that vibe. The possibility is there. I don't know how else to explain it."

"What would it take for it to be that way?"

The answer came to her mind so quickly it left her speechless. *Children*, she thought. *Family. Love.*

She couldn't say those things, so she simply answered, "Healing."

He tugged on her fingers and turned her toward him. "I'm trying."

Her heart squeezed at the honest confession. "I know. And you're doing just fine." She slid closer, wrapping her arms around him and nestling close to his strong, wide chest. "And along the way, you've been healing me, too. For what it's worth, I've loved every moment in your house, from the first time I walked in and saw you with your shirt off."

His arms cinched tightly around her, pulling her close as he laughed. His breath was warm on her hair as they hugged, his body tall and strong and the kind a woman could lean on when she wanted. The brisk wind off the ocean buffeted their bodies, but they stood firm against it, holding on to each other, the moment touching Jess's heart more than any of their more intimate moments. He pulled back a bit and cupped her face in his hands, his smile replaced with a look of wonder. "You've changed everything," he said roughly, and brought his lips down on hers for a kiss.

It was a hell of a time for her to realize she'd broken the ground rules. She'd gone ahead and fallen in love with him. But she wouldn't say it. Not and ruin what they had, when it was so fleeting to begin with.

Bran tried not to think about that kiss as he strolled along the beach with Jess. She stopped now and then to pick up shells, and took off her shoes to dip her toes in the cool water, the light breakers ruffling over her feet before creeping up on the sand and then retreating again. Her hair had come out of its bun and whipped around in the stiff breeze, and her laugh carried to him, making his heart hurt and yearn for things he couldn't have.

He'd seen her feelings on her face even if she hadn't said the words. She had turned away and laughed, running for the beach, but the distraction didn't quite work. He'd seen it, the way her lips fell open the slightest bit with words unsaid and the soft vulnerability and surprise in her eyes. He didn't want to say goodbye to her, not yet. The summer was just coming into its own. There was a good six weeks they could have together if they didn't let emotions get in the way. So thank God she hadn't said what had been written all over her face.

A gull cried overhead, circling above them. He could just pretend it had never happened, that's all. No declarations of love. That was the rule. And despite his suspicions, she hadn't broken it.

Cole, Jeremy and Tori joined them briefly, then as a group they left the beach and made their way back to the golf cart for the return trip to the dock. Bran remained quiet as Cole admitted that he was putting in an offer, and talked excitedly about his plans.

Back on the mainland, Jeremy offered Jess a drive home since they were going to the same place anyway, and that meant Cole and Bran drove back to his house together. Bran was quiet on the way back, until they were nearly at his house. Cole broke from his monologue about the island property and frowned at Bran.

"You know, I wasn't expecting you to have fallen in love this summer."

Bran's head swiveled so fast he nearly put the car in the ditch. "What? I'm not in love. Don't be ridiculous." He chuckled tightly, as if to show how ludicrous of an idea it was, and focused on the road.

But Cole's expression was grim as he continued to stare at Bran. Bran kept glancing over, until Cole finally said, "Dude, it was written all over your face today. You light up when she's around."

"Lighting up is not love, dumbass. It's enjoying someone's company."

"You know, I'd be tempted to say, 'if you say so,' but I'm not, because this is serious, Bran. I want to be happy for you. But I'm not sure you're ready, and she seems like a great person. She doesn't deserve to be hurt."

Bran's temper flared. "If you think Jess and I haven't talked about it, you're wrong. Both of us have our eyes wide open."

And then he thought of the way she'd looked at him today, and his heart stuttered.

They turned onto his lane and made their

way into the garage. The doors echoed in the silence, and Bran opened the door from the garage to the house.

Maybe Cole would let the matter drop.

"Hey, listen. Jeremy and I have been talking about it, too. We're both concerned for you. He said your car has been there overnight. And that you guys went to the city and spent the night earlier this month."

Heat rushed through Bran's chest as irritation flared again. "That is no one's business but ours."

"You're right."

"And it's just sex."

Cole started laughing, putting his hand on the island in the kitchen to brace himself. "Oh," he said, catching his breath. "Bran, you're a horrible liar. I've known you for most of your life. You don't do casual sex. You don't get with a woman without your heart being involved. Brother, you are lying to yourself."

Bran opened his mouth to speak, but Cole held up a hand. "Hey, don't get me wrong. Losing Jennie and Owen was such a horrible, horrible thing, and you deserve to move on and be happy again. I just... I find myself feeling protective of you. I don't want you to get hurt."

Those last words took the heat out of Bran's anger. Cole was a workaholic and he played hard—when he made time for it. But of the three of them, he was the most protective. Like the big brother of the group. As much as no one wanted to admit it, Cole was the glue that bound them together.

And Cole was always there for them...even when he wasn't taking care of himself.

Bran let out a breath. "I can't love her, Cole. There's no danger of that. But I care about her a lot. She's fun and full of life, and she doesn't let me get away with anything. I'm actually writing again, which is a total surprise and a massive relief. But she lives in Chicago. I live here and in New York. We both agreed that this is a temporary thing where we just enjoy each other for the time we have. Because life is short."

Cole went to the fridge and took out two cans of soda. He handed one to Bran and then snapped the top on his own and leaned against the counter. "Okay," he said quietly, "okay. Maybe that's true. But Bran, it's okay if you fall in love with her. You know that, right? I'm worried about you, but it's not *wrong*."

A pit opened up in Bran's stomach as he looked at his friend. How could he make Cole understand when he was finding it hard to understand himself? He wasn't even sure he was capable of being in love. And the look on Jess's face today scared him to death. Not so much because she loved him but because he couldn't feel that way in return.

"I can't, Cole." His voice was low and rough. "My heart won't let me. Maybe it would be easier if I could. Right now I'm trying to look at all the positives. I'm not hurting so much. I'm getting out, I'm writing again. Anything more is a lot to ask for."

"Yet up until she showed up in your life, you weren't doing any of those things. Doesn't that say something to you?"

Bran let out a sigh of resignation. "Yeah," he said, looking past Cole and out at the backyard. "It tells me she deserves someone who can give her a lot more than I can."

And in that moment, he knew he had to stop what was between them.

CHAPTER THIRTEEN

JESS POURED HERSELF some orange juice and tried to decide if she wanted yogurt and berries this morning or something a little more comforting, like toast with butter and jam. She was feeling rather out of sorts after yesterday. The trip to the island had been fun and she'd enjoyed it, but she wasn't so sure about her latest revelation.

She didn't want to be in love with Bran. Up until yesterday, she'd been able to logic her way out of it. But then there was that moment. The moment he'd kissed her, however, something had shifted. Something profound and deep and joyful and sad and terrifying all wrapped up in one ball of emotion.

She loved him, and she wasn't sure if she should break it off now for the sake of self-preservation, or if she should give herself these final weeks as a gift, no matter the end result.

She really wished Ana was here to give her advice and ask her the right questions. Tori was a good friend. Jess had other friends in Chicago. But none like Ana.

A wave of grief threatened to swamp her, so instead she reached for her pillbox, which contained her vitamins and birth control. She stared at the little plastic strip with surprise. How was it that she was on her two sugar pills? It meant she'd get her period anytime. She went to her bedroom to get the next month's supply out of the drawer and put it in the little sleeve. So much had changed since her last cycle. It had literally been only a little over a month since she'd met Bran. Her whole world had been turned upside down.

She was just eating her yogurt when her phone buzzed. It was a text from Bran, explaining that Cole was in town for only a few more days and they were going to spend some time together, but he'd be in touch by the weekend. That was that, then. She'd have time to think and make some decisions before seeing him again.

And in the meantime, she'd paint. There was nothing that helped her work through her problems like putting her heart on canvas.

By Saturday Jess was starting to panic.

She was three days into her new pack of pills and she hadn't had a period at all. Granted, being on the pill made them lighter, but usually on her second sugar pill she started, like clockwork. She laid in bed, staring at the bunk above her, trying not to freak out over the fact that she might be pregnant. Because she'd replayed every detail of her nights with Bran, and had discovered that the morning after their hotel stay she hadn't taken her pill at all. She'd missed it completely. It shouldn't make a difference, but it could. They'd had room service, and she'd come home and had been so distracted that she was sure she'd missed her pill and her vitamins.

She couldn't be pregnant. Oh, Lord, what a mess that would be. She wanted children but not this way. Not with a man who didn't want any. Not on her own with no support. She didn't know how to be a mother.

She threw off the covers. Okay, so that might be putting the cart a long way before the horse. She really couldn't do anything until she took a test. Maybe she just missed for whatever reason. And if it was positive, then she'd figure things out. One step at a time.

The drive to the pharmacy didn't take that long, and Jess figured there was no point in waiting and putting off something that wouldn't change the outcome. So she took one of the tests out of the box and into the bathroom she went. Then she came out and made coffee while waiting the three minutes suggested.

When she went back in and looked at the stick, she let out a huge breath.

Negative.

Her hand shook as she dropped the test in the trash can and sat on top of the toilet for a moment, trying to make sense of her feelings. There was relief, of course, because this was so not the right time and even though she was in love with him, Bran wasn't the right man no matter how much she might want him to be. But there was also disappointment. She thought of all the times she'd held Rose, snuggled her close, and how she longed for her own family. Those feelings were there, too. At least the result had clarified much of her thoughts. She and Bran wanted different things. They were just fooling themselves with ground rules and flings and whatever else. He was a good man. They might even be good for each other. But that didn't mean they had a future.

She was just fixing her coffee when there was a knock on the door and then it opened, as she'd left it unlocked as she usually did during the day. Bran came through the door, a small smile on his face, and a paper bag in his hand. "I went to the bakery," he said, holding up the bag. "And got chocolate croissants."

She wasn't ready for this conversation, so she smiled back and kept it light. "I just made coffee. I'll get you some."

"Sounds good. How've you been?"

What a loaded question. She hesitated and then said, "All right. Has Cole gone back to New York?"

"He left last night."

She handed him a mug. "You had a good visit though, huh?"

Bran nodded. "We did. We caught up about a lot of stuff. This island project of his...it's pretty cool."

"So he's going to do it?"

"Yeah, I think so." Bran's grin was genuinely wide now. "Who knew? The three of us went to school together, live within an hour or so of each other, and now have second homes here in Nova Scotia. You'd almost think we were brothers."

Her heart melted at the genuine affection in his voice. "You are, in all the ways that count. I think it's lovely."

"Thanks. Hey, got any milk or cream for this?"

She'd forgotten he liked his coffee light, and before she could move he'd gone to the fridge, making himself at home as he had the last several times he'd visited. But when he turned around, his face dropped and she realized she'd left the pregnancy test box on the counter.

He put the mug down very quietly.

"Bran, I—"

"Are you pregnant?"

The way he said those three words sent her heart straight to her feet. He made it sound as if the world were truly ending. The last time she'd heard that exact tone, Ana had taken her hand and said, "I have cancer."

Bran was so repulsed by the idea that it wasn't just undesirable. It was a world-ending scenario.

She wanted to say something, but the words wouldn't come together in her mind, let alone out of her mouth. Bran's lips tightened and he picked up the box. "You told me you were on the pill. I bought condoms to double up. And now you're pregnant? I told you I don't want more children. I was very, very clear about that."

His voice wasn't angry. It was worse. It was surgically precise, almost emotionless. She understood he didn't want more kids. She understood that came from grief and that it was his right. He'd been honest from the start. But she also knew that it had taken two of them, and right now it certainly felt as if any blame would have fallen on her, rather than be shared, and that made her angry.

Her voice shook as she replied. "If I were pregnant, we would both bear responsibility. But I'm not, so don't worry, Branson. You're off the hook. You can start breathing again."

"Oh, thank God."

He sounded so relieved that tears stung the backs of her eyes. "Would it have been so bad?" she snapped. "Would me being pregnant be the worst thing in the world to happen?"

He stepped back at the vitriol in her voice. "No. The worst thing in the world to happen is losing a child."

Dammit. Silence fell, harsh and thick. Of course it was. She wasn't that insensitive, even though she'd lashed out. "I'm sorry, Bran. Of course you're right. I didn't mean to…" She didn't know what to say after that. "Look, I'll be honest with you. The night we stayed in Halifax… I forgot to take my pill the next day. I didn't have my period this week on schedule, so I got tests this morning just in case."

"But you're not pregnant."

"No." She lifted her chin a little. "But I think this whole thing, the idea with the ground rules, the summer fling with us going our separate ways with a smile was a little disingenuous on both our parts. I don't think this is going to work anymore."

He blinked. Opened his mouth to say something, then shut it again. Then opened it again, and hesitated. "Jess, I like being with you. You've brought me back to life, you see? I'm writing. I'm looking toward a future rather than drifting aimlessly. We don't have to break it off. We can revise the ground rules—"

"No," she said, firmer now. "No, we can't. Bran, there are two things you don't want. You don't want more children, and you don't want to fall in love. But you see, I do want children someday. And I fell in love. I know that's breaking a rule, but I also know it's a deal breaker anyway. I'm in love with you, and I can't go through the rest of the summer pretending I'm not, only to break up at the end after I get in even deeper." She tried to ignore the catch in her voice. "I don't want to be left again, so we have to do this now."

"Jess," he whispered, running a hand over his face.

"Tell me you haven't been thinking the same thing. In the beginning you couldn't wait to rush over here, to steal moments together. But after the trip to the island earlier this week, you sent one text saying you were hanging with Cole. The three of you are tight, but you guys didn't come over here, and you certainly didn't steal away for a stolen hour. You're scared. So let's be honest, okay? I can't see you anymore. It's too hard."

"Yeah, I've been thinking the same thing. So what? Listen, we don't have to have sex…"

The tears behind her eyes sprang forward and trickled down her cheeks. "Is that what it's been to you? Sex? I don't believe it. Oh, Lord, Bran, this goes so much further than sex. It's about my heart, don't you see? Just being with you, holding your hand, listening to your voice…it all does stuff to me. Intimacy isn't all about the bedroom."

"I know that. Do you think I don't know that? Don't you think that's what I miss about Jennie every day?"

It was his turn to snap, and she swallowed against the growing lump in her throat. It was always going to come down to Jennie, wasn't it? Maybe he didn't compare her to his dead wife when they were together, but he certainly wasn't over her. He didn't want to love again, couldn't love again, because he couldn't let Jennie go.

She couldn't do this anymore. "I'm going to give Tori and Jeremy my notice and go back to my loft in Chicago. My agent is clamoring to do a showing, and I have more than enough work to keep me busy. And you have a book to write."

He came around the counter and took her hand, then lifted his other hand and wiped a tear off her cheek with his thumb. The contact felt so wonderful and sad. After today she wouldn't hear the sound of his voice again, or feel the pad of his thumb, or be able to run her hands through his shaggy locks. She'd be going back to Chicago alone, to the loft she'd shared with Ana, fighting against emptiness all over again. For the briefest of moments, she wished the test had been positive just so she'd have company in that huge empty space. A baby wouldn't leave her. And Bran wasn't leaving her, either. But she was quickly learning that it didn't matter who did the leaving. It all hurt.

"I don't want us to leave things this way," he whispered. "Not angry and hurting. What we've been to each other deserves more than that."

It did, except she was having a hard time moving past the sound of his voice and the hard lines of his face when he'd seen the test box. It left a sour taste that she couldn't quite wish away.

"It does hurt. But I'll be fine. I always am, you see. And we did have a good time, we truly did. It's just time."

He nodded. "Can I kiss you one more time?"

Her heart hadn't actually broken during the

whole conversation. She'd been hurt and she'd been angry, but she hadn't actually felt the moment where the ground seemed to disappear beneath her feet and left this sense of…emptiness. But now…she knew it was for the best, and yet she wanted him to tell her that she was wrong; that he had fallen in love with her too and they could work it out.

She'd always been a stupid dreamer like that.

Her lips trembled as he bent his head and touched his mouth to hers, then pressed his forehead against hers for a long moment while his hands gripped her upper arms.

"I'm sorry," he whispered. "I'm sorry I can't give you what you want."

He let her go and turned away, and without looking back went through the door, down the steps and to his car.

Every cell in her body begged her to go after him and tell him it didn't matter.

But it did matter. And it was for the best. Because she deserved someone who loved her unreservedly.

And that wasn't him, no matter how much she wanted it to be.

CHAPTER FOURTEEN

BRAN VENTURED OUT to the lighthouse to survey the latest work. It was coming along nicely, now that the restoration had begun. The foundation had been sound, but there'd been work to do at the top, including replacing the platform and making everything airtight. The door was replaced with a replica of the old one, and fresh paint would go on early next week.

The biggest change, however, was the addition of windows on the bottom level. Now when he went inside, beams of light lit the interior, making the empty space bright and cheery.

Except nothing was very cheery at all.

He ran his finger over the top of the woodstove, remembering the day Jess had been here and she'd cautioned him not to open the stove door in case there were mice. He smiled a little at the memory, but sadness made his heart heavy. He missed her. His days had gone back to the routine of one after another, little variation, too much time on his own.

The writing was there now, at least, and he'd sent off an opening and general synopsis to his agent, who'd responded with relief. Bran wasn't a lot of things, but he was still a writer, thank God. Even if the sunshine seemed to have disappeared from his life, he was back in the land of the living.

It just seemed so very bland and pointless without her.

Despondent, he went back to the house and made himself a coffee, then wandered to the den. He booted up his laptop and then, missing her more than usual, opened the browser and went to her website.

It had been updated.

She had a show opening in late October in Chicago. A recent photo showed her laughing, her face alight with happiness and her sunshiny hair gleaming. It hit him right in the gut. Of course she was happy. He was glad. But he was resentful, too. That she'd clearly moved on and he was still…here. Moping half the time and writing the other.

But this was what he'd wanted. What he'd chosen.

His attention was diverted by a car coming up the driveway—Jeremy's Jaguar. Bran closed the window and shut the laptop, preparing himself for a visit. Cole would be closing on the island property soon, and then the three of them had made a promise to spend a weekend after the possession date, a guys' weekend with some deep-sea fishing, maybe some rounds of pool in the games room, and unhealthy food like chicken wings and pizza. Bran was looking forward to it.

Anything to be able to stop thinking about her all the time.

He opened the door for Jeremy, and immediately had a moment of alarm. The man looked like he'd hardly slept. His hair stuck up on one side, and his eyes were red.

"What's happened?" Bran asked, his heart freezing.

"Rose is sick. She's in Halifax at the children's hospital right now, but I've just spent twenty-four hours there and came home to get stuff to take back. Except... I can't go in the house, Bran. I didn't know where else to go."

Bran took a deep breath. While memories threatened to overwhelm him, he pushed them aside. His best friend needed him, and Bran knew the fear and shock Jeremy was going through. "Is Tori okay?"

Jeremy nodded. "She's fine. Still at the hospital. We didn't want to leave Rose alone, and there was no way I was going to be able to tear Tori away, so…"

His voice trailed off, weak and shaky.

"It's okay. You need to pick up what, clothes? Toiletries? Maybe some food for Tori, so she keeps eating?"

Jeremy nodded, his expression one of exhaustion and misery. "Yes, all of those things."

"I'll help." He put his hand on Jeremy's shoulder. "You don't have to do this alone, okay?"

Jeremy nodded. "I'm sorry, bro. I know this is hard for you—"

"Not as much as it used to be. I'm okay. I can deal. Promise."

He realized it was true as he grabbed his wallet and keys. Three months ago—even two—he would have run in the other direction. Not now. He took Jeremy's keys from him and drove them over to the house, then waited while Jeremy gathered clothes and personal items. Bran walked over to the sofa and paused, staring down at a little yellow bunny on the cushions. He remembered that bunny. Jess had bought it during one of their trips to the market.

Things were suddenly very quiet, so Bran braced himself and made his way upstairs to check on his friend. He found Jeremy in the nursery, sitting in a rocking chair and holding a blanket in his hands. He wasn't crying, but

Bran knew that meant nothing. He was hurting on the inside, and he was scared.

"Do they know what's wrong with her?" Bran finally asked, keeping his voice as calm as possible.

"Measles. Something about how she could have picked them up at her last checkup, but she's too little for the vaccine yet." His tortured gaze met Bran's. "Babies can die from measles, Bran."

"I know. But she's at the hospital and getting great care, right?"

Jeremy nodded.

"Okay. So let's put this stuff in the car and get to Halifax so you can give Tori a break. All right?"

Jeremy nodded. "Yeah. Yeah, let's go."

As Jeremy got up, Bran noticed a framed picture on the wall. It was a sketch, and one of Jess's, he was sure of it. Of Rose, in a little bonnet, bundled up and in presumably Tori's arms. A lump formed in his throat. That precious little girl, who smiled and gurgled at her father's silly faces, who looked at her mother so adoringly, who had studied him with such wide-eyed curiosity the night of the card game as he'd picked her up for the first time.

His best friend would not lose his daughter the way he'd lost Owen.

They packed the two bags in the car, and Bran offered to drive so Jeremy could rest. They had barely hit the highway when Jeremy fell asleep, and Bran was glad of it. He'd likely been awake all night, worrying about Rose and Tori. Bran remembered one time when Owen had got a cold and struggled to breathe so much. There'd been sleepless nights, but he'd also hated to see Jennie so exhausted and worried.

Bran found his way to the children's hospital and pulled into the parking garage, waking Jeremy as he rolled down the window for the parking stub. "We're here, buddy."

"I didn't mean to sleep. Sorry."

"Don't be. You needed the rest. Come on, I'll go in with you. Is there someplace inside where we can grab you and Tori some food? Coffee?"

Jeremy nodded. "Yeah. I don't know if Tori will eat, but…"

"Tea," Bran suggested. "She drinks tea a lot, right? Get her tea and a sandwich she can pick at. It's your job to make sure she takes care of herself. And you can't do that if you don't look after yourself, too."

"I'm fine."

"Humor me."

They spent precious minutes picking up sandwiches and drinks, and then Bran carried the overnight bags in his hands as Jeremy hit the elevator button taking them to the correct floor. Bran's pulse accelerated as they headed for the isolation unit; he hated hospitals, and the memories bubbled to the surface simply from the sounds and the smell that was so peculiar to hospitals. But he carried on, knowing that for months Jeremy had been there for him, and it was his turn to repay the favor.

Poor little Rose was in isolation since she was so contagious. Once they arrived, Tori came out, shedding her mask and gown. She looked like hell. Her hair was pulled back in a ponytail, and there were dark circles under her eyes. She appeared to have slept in her clothes, but the relief on her face when she saw Jeremy lit up the room. Bran felt a strange emotion wash over him. It was like just being in the same room together made everything okay. He'd felt that not long ago, with Jess. She hadn't had to do anything but be there and smile, and the world was forever changed.

He was forever changed.

He put the bags down and went forward to give Tori a hug. "Hello, little mama," he said softly, giving her a squeeze. "How's she doing?"

"They're giving her fluids through an IV and stuff to bring down her fever. We just keep hoping there aren't complications like—" she took a breath, swallowed, got herself together again "—like encephalitis."

"She's a tough cookie. And Jeremy has food for you."

"I'm not hungry."

"Then save the sandwich for later and drink some tea. He got mint, the kind you like."

She looked up, and Jeremy was holding out the paper cup. "I got a large. You need to look after yourself too, honey. You haven't slept."

"Neither have you."

He smiled a little. "I slept in the car while Bran drove."

Bran peeked into the room and clenched his teeth. He couldn't see anything, but he imagined poor little Rose, blotchy and red, sleeping while an IV was taped to her, delivering fluids and medication. No little one should have to go through such a thing.

Tori sat down and peeled the top back on the tea. The scent of peppermint filled the air. "I don't want to be out here too long. I keep thinking she has to know that we're there. I've been singing to her."

"Of course she knows you're there." Bran sat down next to Jeremy, and reached for the bag of sandwiches. "Here, you two. Seriously, eat something. And while you're doing that, I'm going to book you a hotel room nearby. Even if you have to sleep in shifts, it'll give you a base until she's able to go home. You can get some good rest and have a hot shower."

"Bran, you don't have to do that."

He leaned forward and met Jeremy's eyes, and finally said something he should have said long ago. "When I needed you, you were there. Bullying me into eating and sleeping and showering. Sitting with me. This is a very small thing, Jer. Let me do it for you."

Jeremy nodded. "Okay."

"Do you need anything else? Is there anything I can do?"

"Not right now. Thank you, Bran."

He excused himself and went to a nearby lounge to make accommodation arrangements, giving Jeremy and Tori time alone. His thumbs hovered over the keypad, knowing he should send the message and afraid to all the same. He hadn't had contact with Jess since that day at the boathouse when they'd called it quits.

Still, she'd want to know.

Before he could reconsider, he typed rapidly.

Jess, just letting you know that Rose is in the hospital in Halifax with the measles. I'm here with Jeremy and Tori. Bran.

He sat back in the chair and replayed that

morning in his mind. He'd been such an ass. Handled things all wrong just because seeing the pregnancy test box had scared him out of his wits. He'd known they had to break it off, but not like that. He'd wanted to explain that she deserved so much more. That she was wonderful and needed someone who could give her all of himself. Give her the family she wanted. And Lord, not ask her to take on so much baggage. Instead, he'd jumped down her throat and it had just been…awful.

He regretted that more than anything. That their beautiful friendship had ended with harsh words and hurt feelings. It seemed their relationship deserved a better ending.

His phone vibrated in his hand, and he looked at the screen. Jess had replied.

Oh, no! Is she okay? I'll call Tori. She must be so distressed.

There was a pause, and then another quick message.

I appreciate you telling me, Bran.

He didn't know what to say after that. Anything would either be too much or not enough. He tucked the phone back in his pocket and sat for a long time, replaying old thoughts in his head. Some made sense but others…others did not. What did that mean for his future? Could he truly go through life with a couple of friends and a laptop for company?

He'd missed her every single day.

Eventually he made his way back to the unit. Tori was leaned against Jeremy's shoulder, her eyes closed and breathing deep.

"I'll go so she can rest."

"Stay a minute. She'll sleep for a while now. The tea helped her relax."

They kept their voices low, and Jeremy adjusted a little so that the angle of Tori's neck was a little gentler. Then he looked up at Bran. "You and Jess. What happened?"

Bran swallowed. Thought about how happy he'd been just to see her impersonal text minutes earlier. "I wasn't ready. And she had a pregnancy scare."

"Oh, man. That sent you running for the hills, huh."

"Considering the current situation, I'm not sure you want to talk about Owen."

Jeremy nodded slowly, but then met Bran's eyes. "I'm a wreck, it's true. That little girl… and her mother…they changed my life. I can't imagine…no, that's not true. I can imagine, and it scares me to death. So I think I understand. Yours isn't just imagination. You've lived through it and would rather do anything than go through it again."

That Jeremy understood so completely came as a relief. "Yeah. There's just one problem, Jer."

"What's that?"

"I'm in love with her."

Jeremy let out a huge breath. "Well, doesn't that make the cheese more binding."

They both laughed a little.

"I couldn't admit it when she was here. I mean it when I say I wasn't ready. I wasn't over Jennie. I don't know if I'll ever be over Jennie. How is that fair?"

Jeremy frowned. "I'm not sure this is ever anything you are 'over.' I think it's a decision to leave it in the past, and be brave enough to embrace a future. It's a big thing."

"It's a huge thing. She wants a family, Jer. And she should have one. You've seen her with Rose. She loves that little girl. She should have babies of her own if that's what she wants. And I just don't know."

"All love carries risks."

"I know."

"And rewards. But only you can decide where that balance lies. If being without her is easier than taking the risk, then you know letting her go was the right thing."

"But if it's not?"

Jeremy shrugged. "You have to sort that out on your own. All I'm going to say is that I loved Jennie, but Jess had a way of making you smile that was just…different. There's no question in my mind that she fell in love with you."

Tori shifted and he moved with her, smoothing her hair off her face while she slept on. Bran marveled at the tenderness he saw in his friend's expression.

"Love changes a person, you know?" Jeremy looked away from his wife's face and smiled. "It made me a better man. It made me want things I didn't feel worthy of asking, but somehow…she makes it right. You found it once, Bran. If you are lucky enough to have found it a second time, think long and hard before letting it slip away."

CHAPTER FIFTEEN

JESS HAD NEVER been so glad for air-conditioning in her life.

Chicago was stifling. A late July heat wave was making things miserable, and she cringed to think of her power bill with how much her AC was running, but at least she was comfortable. Most of the time.

Living alone had never been this difficult. Ana had been the one to move into the loft with her, taking the second bedroom and bringing her boundless energy and kindness with her. After she'd gone, it had been hard to live in the apartment without hearing Ana's voice, singing in the shower, or the way she'd stay up on Saturdays watching old movies.

But this loneliness was different. Because it wasn't the loft that was quiet and lonely, it was her whole life. It was like taking one of her paintings and suddenly only seeing it in black and white. There was a vibrancy missing that she knew had one cause: Bran.

She missed him. It seemed impossible; they'd been together such a short time. But time didn't matter. What was time, anyway? Measurable in months, days, hours, minutes...and yet it moved slowly and quickly. Her time in Nova Scotia had been too short, and now her days were too long. And yet the clock ticked on at the same pace.

So she worked. She buried herself in it, putting all her feelings and thoughts and longings and regrets on canvas. It was the neglected door and the determined daisies, the lighthouse strong and sure, and the waves and wind that battered it relentlessly. It was a long, white beach that stretched on forever, and a man standing on a bluff overlooking the ocean, lost.

Her agent had seen most of what she'd done and raved over it. Jess had come away from the meeting glad he was happy, but personally caring little about the commercial appeal of it and more concerned with the process.

The only thing she could think to do was paint him out of her heart. So far she wasn't succeeding.

Had she been wrong to leave? Should she have given him more time? Maybe. Though in her heart she knew staying would have just prolonged the inevitable.

A quick glance at the clock on the microwave showed just after one o'clock, so she decided it was as good a time as any for a break. She turned on the kettle to make coffee. She'd picked up some bagels at the market a few days ago, so she popped one in the toaster. A bagel with cream cheese would suffice for lunch.

The kettle had just boiled and she'd poured the water into the press when a knock sounded at the door.

She frowned. A courier, maybe? She certainly wasn't expecting anyone. She padded to the door in her bare feet and peeked through the hole to see who was there.

Bran.

Her paint-stained fingers flew to her mouth. What was he doing here? Her first thought was that something had happened to Rose. Oh, God, she hoped not. But would he fly all the way here to deliver that news?

The only other option was that he was here for her. And that was…unbelievable. Considering how they'd left things.

She opened the door, curiosity getting the better of her.

His gaze swept over her, top to bottom to top again, and a smile bloomed on his face. "You look wonderful," he said. His voice held a note of reverence that touched her deeply, and she bit down on her lip. And in the next moment she was in his arms, in the middle of the biggest bear hug she could ever remember.

It was a shock and confusing as heck, but she went with it, because it was so damned good to see him again and hold him close. The scent that was uniquely Bran—soap and aftershave and sea air. How could he smell like the sea after sitting on a plane?

"You feel so good," he said close to her ear, sending shivers down her body. "God, I've missed you."

He loosened his hold and she leaned back so she could see his face, trying not to be so glad to see him. "What are you doing here? Is Rose okay?" He'd cut his hair, she noticed. Not super short, but the shaggy locks were tamed and his beard was precisely trimmed. It was sexy as anything.

"That little bean is just about perfect. She's very close to rolling over."

Oh, bless him. He called Rose a little bean. Why did he have to be so…everything?

She wilted in relief. "Okay, good. Because I thought for a minute you'd come to tell me that…" She hesitated. "I'm sorry. I shouldn't bring stuff like that up."

"No, it's okay. She was really sick, but she's okay now. Full recovery. And that's not why I'm here. But maybe we could go inside and close the door? It's hot as blazes out here, and you're letting all your lovely cool air out."

He wasn't wrong, so she stepped back and once they were clear of the threshold, shut the door. It was a relief to be out of the midday heat.

"Do you want coffee? I just made some. It's likely to be strong now. I poured the water in my press the moment you knocked."

"Coffee sounds great."

She led the way to the kitchen, which was about a quarter of the size of the one in his house and still held a small dining set. Heart pounding, fingers trembling, she got two mugs out of the cabinet and then pushed down the plunger in the press, pouring strong brew in each cup.

She looked up at him. "There's milk in the fridge."

His gaze held hers. Coffee and milk had been the catalyst on that last fateful day. But now he calmly went to the refrigerator, took out a carton of milk put it on the counter.

"I'm sorry, Jess. For all the things I said that day."

"Me, too. I mean... I knew we had to end, but that wasn't how I wanted it to happen."

"Do you think it ever would have been parting with a kiss and a fond farewell and a 'thanks for the memories'?" he asked. He came a step closer. "Because I think it was always going to be messy. I'm not sure it can be avoided when two people love each other."

She was holding out his mug for him to take when he said those words, and suddenly she couldn't move. Her hand started to shake. He reached out and took the mug and then set it down on the table.

"You heard me right. You said you loved me that day, and I did not. I didn't think I could. I thought it was impossible. But the truth is, I was already in love with you and too scared to admit it to myself. It was easier to say I'd never love anyone again. There was protection in it."

"You weren't ready. I knew that. It's why I had to go."

"I know, sweetheart. I know."

This wasn't happening. He wasn't here, in her kitchen, saying all these wonderful things. Panic threaded through her veins. She'd thought she'd known what she wanted. But it turned out she didn't know anything. Oh, how smug she'd been.

"What changed?" she asked, trying and failing to keep the tremor out of her voice.

"Rose. And Jeremy. And me being a lonely,

grumpy man whose closest relationship is with his laptop. And I wouldn't even have that if it weren't for you." He took her hand. "Come, sit. Let me explain, and then you can decide what you want to do with me."

Oh, she knew what she wanted to do with him. That hadn't changed. But this was about more than their physical compatibility. It always had been.

He held her hand as she across from him. "When Rose got sick, Jeremy came for me. He was a wreck. He's my best friend. Of course I was going to be there for him. And walking into that hospital made me face a lot of things. But it also helped me realize that I've healed a lot. Jennie and Owen—they're a part of my past that will always be in my heart. But I can't keep living there. It's not living at all, and after I met you, I discovered I actually do want to live again."

"Oh, Bran…"

"And then Jeremy gave me a bit of a talking-to. And I've been thinking for a while now about what I want my life to look like. I've come to the conclusion that I don't much care, as long as you're in it."

Tears threatened to spill over. "You really mean that."

"I do." He squeezed her fingers. "Loving

again terrifies me, I'm not gonna lie. But being without you scares me more. I never thought I'd ever find this again. That there'd be someone I couldn't live without." He hesitated a moment, licked his lips and then said, "You told me once that the people that you loved had all left you. When I remembered that, I realized why you sent me away that day. You walked away first so I wouldn't, didn't you?"

The tears did spill over then. It was the secret wound she'd only ever shared with two people—him and Ana. And Ana was gone now. She nodded. "I suppose I did." She sniffled and wiped her fingers over her cheeks. "God, I'm sorry. I don't mean to cry."

"It's okay. I hurt you. We hurt each other because we were scared. I'm still scared, Jess. But I'm here. And I'm staying, if you'll have me."

Silence fell in the tiny kitchen. "What do you mean, staying?"

He reached out and cupped her cheek tenderly. "I mean, you get to decide. You have a life here. I can write anywhere. I have a place in New York and the house in Nova Scotia and wherever you want to be, that's where we'll go. All I need is an internet connection, a supply of coffee and you."

He was offering her everything. She loved this loft, but she loved a lot of things. And there was still one thing they hadn't talked about. A very big, very important thing.

"What about children?"

He met her gaze evenly. "I miss being a father. It's going to scare me to death, but, yes. Yes, to a family. I look at Jeremy and Tori, and it's something that's missing in my heart. I'll always have a spot for Owen. But I won't love our babies any less, Jess."

Now he really was giving her everything. She stood and went over to him, sitting on his knees, wrapping her arms around his shoulders as she started to cry for real. He was here. He loved her. He wanted babies. And Bran... she knew in the deepest parts of her heart and soul that he was not the kind of man to leave once he'd promised to stay. Not if he had any choice in the matter. And life didn't have guarantees, did it?

But it certainly had wishes and dreams come true.

"Do you know what I want the most?" she said, holding him close.

"What?"

"I want to go home."

EPILOGUE

THE CHICAGO AIR had lost the summer heat, and the breeze was now cool and brisk in the first week of November. Bran held Jess's hand as they entered the gallery, and then gave her a kiss as Jack rushed over and took her away to do artisty things. Bran knew the drill; he'd done the same during signings and events, and he was thrilled to see Jess enjoying so much success.

She was so beautiful tonight, in a long black dress that hugged her curves and her hair up in the topknot he'd come to love so much. Her freckles were hidden by makeup, and her lips were a pretty shade of pink. She'd told him, back in the hotel room, that she'd forbidden the esthetician from using false eyelashes. He'd laughed and kissed her, nearly ruining the careful makeup job.

There'd be time enough for that later.

Instead, he accepted a rare glass of champagne and took his time wandering through the gallery. The collection was small but beautiful; he was so stinkin' proud of what she'd accomplished. And these paintings would always be special to him. It was like a visual diary of how he'd fallen in love with Jess. Or as she was known tonight, *the* Jessica Blundon.

There were three paintings in black and white that he thought were stunning. One was of the reflectors of the lighthouse lamp, and so very different from her other works. A second one was a fishing boat, tied to a dock. And the third made him catch his breath. It was him. Standing on the bluff by the lighthouse, looking out over a rough sea. He looked so…lonely. Bereft. He understood why she'd done it in black and white.

An arm slid through his, and she pressed up against him. "Hello, handsome."

"Hello, famous artist. This one…wow, Jess."

"I took a pic of that the first day, when you kicked me off the property," she said softly. "Something about you just drew me in. I never believed you were an angry old troll."

He snorted and laughed, and looked down at her. She shared an impish smile with him that made him warm all over.

The last months had been nothing short of amazing. Jess had gone back to Nova Scotia with him, staying at his house, and he'd turned the lighthouse into a studio for her. He'd finished the draft of his book, and they were making a stop in New York on the way home so he could meet with his agent and editor. He'd sold his brownstone there that he'd shared with Jennie, and that had been hard, but Jeremy was going to hook them up with a new property that was just for them.

Life was moving forward, and he was happy.

Unlike the man in the painting. But instead of being sad, it made him realize how far he'd come, thanks to the love of the wonderful woman at his side.

"Come with me for a moment," she said, removing her arm from his and reaching for his hand instead. "There's something I want you to see."

She led him to the other side of the gallery, where a lone painting was displayed. He stopped and stared. It was the same painting—with him on the bluff—but it was in full color, rich and vibrant. The sea wasn't angry; the waves were joyous and playful, and the grass and flowers waved in bright sunlight next to a pristine white lighthouse. Before and after.

But what truly made it different was that he wasn't alone in this one. A woman was beside him. She was beside him, in a flowy dress and her hair up and…

And in between them was a small child, holding on to their hands.

"I was going to call this one *Dreams*," she said. "And then I decided it was something else."

"What?" he asked, his throat tight and his heart full.

"Future."

He stepped closer. The little silver plaque beneath it had *Future* inscribed. And there was a tag on it that said "Not for sale."

"Jess?"

"I'm not selling this one. It's our future, Bran."

He stared into her eyes. "Are you saying…"

She put her hand to her still-flat stomach, but a smile broke out on her face and he swore she lit up like a candle.

"I took the test last week. Barely, but yes, I'm pregnant."

He started to laugh. He couldn't help it. It was a joyful expression of happiness and disbelief, mostly that he could be this lucky. "It's funny?" she asked, raising an eyebrow.

"It's unbelievable," he confirmed, and pressed a quick kiss to her lips. "Look, I was going to do this whole big thing after your showing, but I think this is the right time." He reached into his suit jacket and took out a blue box. "I love you, Jess. I don't know that I believed in angels until you showed up at my lighthouse, being all sassy and beautiful. But if there are angels, you're mine. Will you marry me?"

She nodded. He put the ring on her finger, then pulled her close, amazed and awed that their baby was between them right now.

Jeremy was right after all. Not everyone got lucky a second time around. Now that he had, he was never going to let her go.

* * * * *

If you missed the previous story in
South Shore Billionaires trilogy,
check out

Christmas Baby for the Billionaire

And look out for the next book
Coming soon!

If you enjoyed this story,
check out these other great reads
from Donna Alward

Summer Escape with the Tycoon
Secret Millionaire for the Surrogate
Best Man for the Wedding Planner

All available now!